ABOUT THE AUTHOR

Claire Merchant is an Australian author and storyteller. She is best known for her collection of fantasy, contemporary, and romance novels set in fictional South Coast. In 2018, Claire was voted one of the '50 Great Writers You Should Be Reading' by The Authors Show.

MISTRY AT DAWN

...Such is Life

ALSO BY CLAIRE MERCHANT

Mistry by Moonlight

South Coast Son

Foresight

Forever Ruby

Knowing Nora

Midnight Mistry

A Lady Born, A Pirate Bred

Christian and Layla

Finding Hope

Dreaming of Reality

Linger

Heart Strings

Daughter Departed

Ebony Rose

Light and Shadow: The Story of Luna Lake

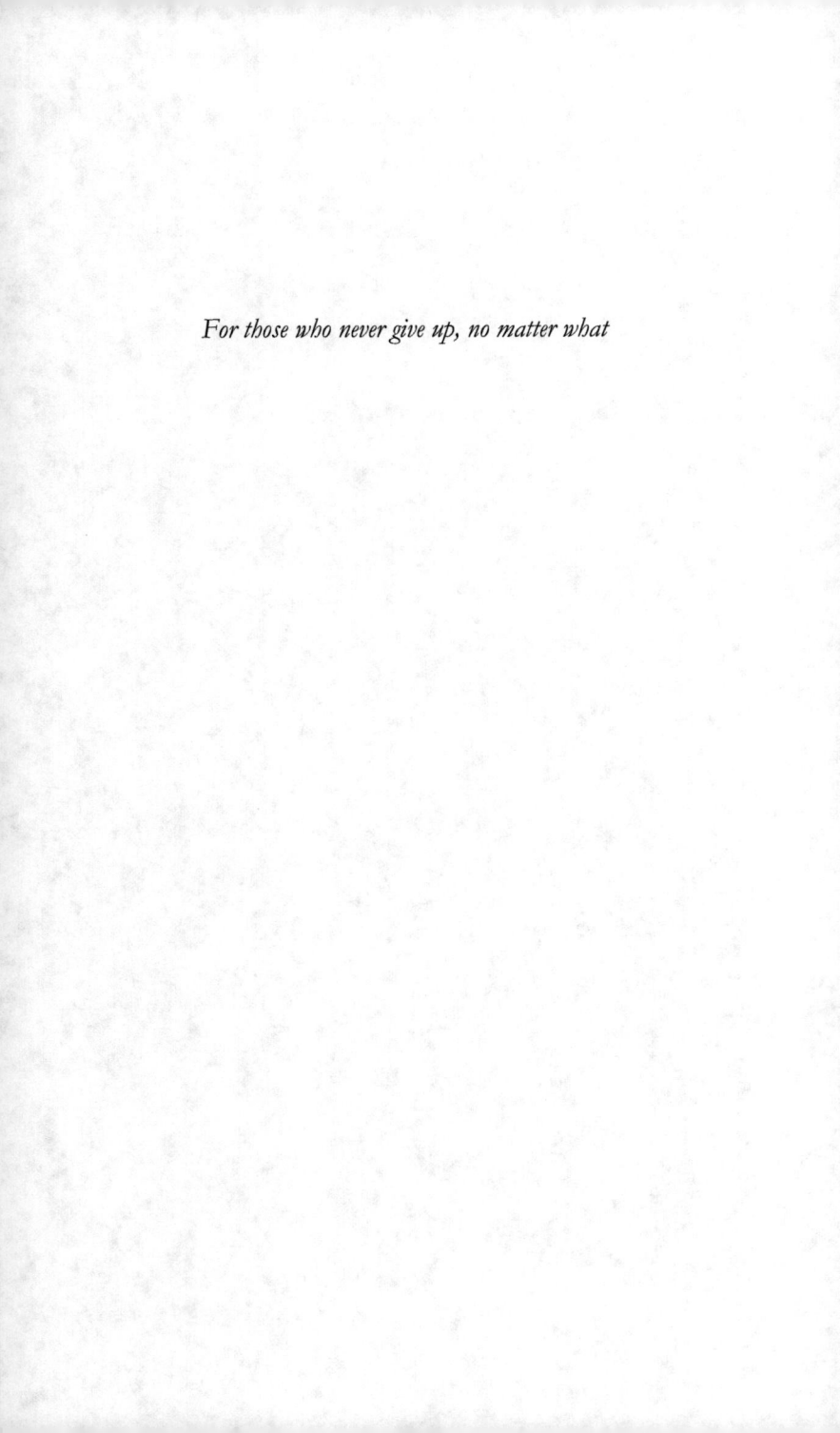

For those who never give up, no matter what

Acknowledgements

Thank *you*.

Thank you for picking up this book and breathing life into it. Taylor Mistry's story may have started with me, but it lives on with you. Thank you for caring about Taylor and Harper, Cole and Ruby, Sal, Jesse, Brandon, and even Hunter. These characters are very much a part of my life, and I'm glad that they could be a part of yours too.

Thank you to my teachers and mentors at Yidarra Catholic Primary School, Corpus Christi College, and The University of Notre Dame Australia, Fremantle (or as I like to think of it, South Coast University). Knowledge is power so thank you for sharing yours with me.

Thank you to my angels for looking out for me. Without you, I don't know where I would be.

Last but not least, thank you to my family and friends for all your love and support. I'm so blessed to have you. You truly make life worth living.

Be yourself. Be gracious. Be kind.
Such is fate.

Claire x

Preface
Final Consequence

I believe in fate.

I am no stranger to death.

I know what it means to fear for my life.

But it was nothing like I was experiencing now.

I thought that after going through times that seemed darker than midnight that surely, surely, the light of dawn was in sight. But the only glow that I saw now was the glow of death, the symbol of an ending life.

I could feel the blood dripping down my skin as the knife sank into my flesh. I wasn't sure what was worse, the pain of the sharp point that cut into me, or knowing that those who were witnessing it could not come to my aid. But as I lay there, contemplating the events that had passed, I realised that I didn't want them to. I didn't want anyone else to experience pain because of me. I didn't want them to have to endure any similar torture to the kind that I was being put through.

The silver blade had been intended for me, and although I didn't want to die, even I had to accept that maybe this was what it had all been building up to. Maybe this was my fate.

The knife glided across my skin and a fresh seeping string of red liquid trickled down. I gritted my teeth to suppress the satisfaction that my scream may bring to my torturer.

"Please," someone said. I couldn't quite pick who spoke, but the voice was hushed and rational. "There is no reason to torture her."

"I can think of a few."

The blade glided across my collarbone, and I clenched my jaw harder. The point moved to my cheek, and with a flick of a wrist, another slice was made, another drop of blood wasted.

I tried to breathe as my head was forced back by my hair. A tear trickled down my face as more voices of protest sounded around the room.

I wondered how much more I could take before my body shut down.

The tip of the knife sank into my stomach, and as it went in deeper, I couldn't contain my scream any more. I felt the blade withdraw and then it crossed my vision. The blood, my blood, dropped off the tip and onto my already bloodstained skin.

I blinked back tears.

"Where in God's name is Harper?"

Such is life.

Phase One

The Death Cry

The Moon was a ghost in the sky, covered by a wispy breath of cloud. It wasn't a Full Moon. It wasn't even a Waning Gibbous, which occurred the night after a Full Moon. It was the Last Quarter, a Half Moon ascending on to my favourite time of the month when there was no Moon in the sky. A New Moon was the safest time for me, and for my werewolf-boyfriend, Harper. Of course, his safety was more my concern now when the Moon was at its apex. Ever since I'd saved him, and consequently been marked by a banshee, then hunted by supernatural creatures and accidentally killed the banshee that marked me, I had inherited the supernatural reaper job myself. So every Full Moon, I turned into the screaming white woman with silver-embedded nails and hunted my prey to restore the natural balance to those who were supernatural in South Coast. It had been seven days since the last Full Moon, and the first time that I'd changed. Seven days since I had attacked Harper's friend, Hunter, and killed her cougar-shifting mate, André. His light had shone too bright, and as a banshee, that was my way of knowing that he'd outstayed his welcome and outlived his lifespan. His time was up, so his glow had to be extinguished. I didn't want to kill him, but I didn't have a choice. I had no control over it. That lack of control had been a fear of mine since learning my fate. I didn't so much fear death as I did cause death for others. Especially Harper.

When I first started seeing the lifespan glows in the supernatural, it confused me to notice that Harper's glow had begun to flicker.

We suspected that it was caused by him escaping the grips of death by firstly being saved by me, and then secondly being healed by his godfather, Rob's blood. Rob was a Shadow Weaver, which was the dark magic breed that existed in South Coast. They were the warm conjurers, who could create fire and lightning, heal themselves, and poison people with a touch. They could become invisible, manipulate objects via telekinesis, and teleport with a puff of smoke. They were the natural enemies of the Light Lacers who were, on the contrary, cold. Lacers could create water and ice, grow plants, breath underwater, move at super speed, and teleport objects and themselves via a shimmery light. I hadn't met any Light Lacers, because they were rare and almost extinct as a breed. Apparently, the feud between them and Weavers had ensured that the few who were left stayed hidden for their own preservation. I didn't have a lot to do with the magic breeds, only really Rob's daughter, Eden, who seemed to overstay her welcome. But I would be eternally grateful to their existence purely for the fact that it meant that Harper was still alive. Even if it meant that he wasn't quite the same after it.

Every time his body had needed to heal itself, his flickering light began to dim even more. It was only made worse when I attacked Hunter and André, and he was stabbed with the silver

14

hunter's dagger that was intended for me. He had intercepted Hunter's aim, which made his light all but disappear. Our mutual friend and vampire, Doctor Cole Frost, had predicted that one more major wound would extinguish his glow all together, activating his constant healing capacity to make him all but immortal, or at least age resistant. Harper had hoped that if he extinguished his glow, that it would mean that he would also extinguish himself from my hit-list each Full Moon. So, with the tip of the same silver hunter's dagger that I had drawn from his shoulder on the first night we'd met, he had made the sacrifice of immortality so I would not face being responsible for his demise.

The silver dagger was unique, having been created by a Shadow Weaver melting the silver into form, and a Light Lacer setting it. The opposing magical forces uniting made it the only weapon that could kill me, a banshee. But any silver could still harm or kill Harper if struck true enough. It was only time that was no longer the enemy, or so we assumed. I couldn't see Harper's glow any more, but that didn't mean much. It was all just scientific guessing at this stage.

The other supernatural beings that I knew didn't really have a glow – the vampires were undead immortals, unable to die unless staked with silver. Eden, as a Shadow Weaver, was apparently able to mask herself with magic. Then there was Sal. Salvatore Vincent, the grim reaper, or just reaper as he much preferred. Sal was an Italian philosophy student at South Coast University, who also happened to be one of the most sarcastic and annoying people that I'd ever met. He did know a lot about death though and had taken me along on one of his reaps once.

That was before I'd changed into a full banshee myself, and the pain went along with his job to relive the human suffering was crippling. As a reaper, Sal saw darkness in humans when they were close to death. He'd seen that darkness in my twin brother's girlfriend, Ashley, who had died the same night that I had killed André while in banshee form. Sal had become a reaper by exchanging his death with the reaper that transitioned his family into the afterlife. As a result, he was technically dead, so his light was non-existent. The only other supernatural creature that I knew was Hunter, and she had made herself scarce after the Full Moon a week ago. I expected her to come back for her revenge in due course since I had been the reason for André's death, and her stabbing Harper, who I was convinced that she was still harbouring feelings for.

It didn't matter though. I knew that Harper loved me and, well, I could never imagine loving him any less.

"Your phone is ringing," Harper whispered into my neck in his silky French-English accent. We were curled up together on a blanket on the esplanade near South Coast University. It wasn't the smartest idea to be there after dark, but there wasn't much around that could harm us.

"My phone is on silent," I sighed.

"I can still hear it."

I rolled my eyes and twisted around to my bag. I fossicked around and felt the vibration as I pulled it out. It was my twin brother, Jesse.

"Jess?" I said.

"*Hey, Tay,*" Jesse croaked. His voice seemed flat since Ashley's death, dull.

"Is something wrong?"

"I... no. I just wanted to let you know that I'm back from Half Moon Bay, but I won't be home when you get home. If you get home tonight, that is."

I glanced at Harper who was looking at me with his beautiful olive-green eyes.

"Did you get called back to work?" I asked. Jesse was an intern doctor, following the footsteps of my father, Doctor Jackson Mistry. I had gone in another direction to my family and was studying veterinary medicine. I suppose we were all reasonably scientific – excluding my mother, Charlie, who was a dance teacher.

"No, I'm not working. I'm just going out."

"With Brandon?" I asked. Brandon was Jesse's best friend – and had been since we were twelve. I used to have a crush on him growing up, but that was when I was overweight and overlooked. It was only after I'd lost twenty-two kilos that his head started to turn in my direction, but by then, I'd had my hands full with an Italian wolf-hunter, and a French-English werewolf. Funnily enough, stranger things had happened since then.

"No, not Brandon, another friend. Brandon is meeting up with Eden, I think."

"Didn't he and Eden break up? Did I miss something? Are they back together?"

"Probably," he sighed. "Apparently."

I bit my lip. My brother wasn't usually this impatient with me. I paused, waiting for him to say more, but there was only silence, so I guessed that meant that he wasn't going to.

"So when did you get back, Jess?" I asked. "Weren't you supposed to be there another few days? You planned for a week, right?"

There was another pause. "*Right, a week. But we decided, I, we decided to come back early.*"

I wasn't used to feeling like he was keeping things from me. I wasn't one to talk since he didn't know any of the mystical mystery surrounding me, but I couldn't help but feel frustrated by it. I wanted to help him, and I couldn't do that if he weren't being honest with me.

"Okay, well I'll see you when I see you then," I said. My teeth sank into my lower lip. "Probably tomorrow morning... or afternoon."

"*Okay. Sure.*"

I frowned. "Jess?"

"*Yes, Taylor?*"

"Is everything okay?" I asked. "I mean, are you okay?"

He exhaled. "*Nothing is okay. Not without her.*"

Ashley.

He had taken her death really hard. Understandably so.

"I love you, Jesse. Be safe, okay?" I said.

"*Sure, you too. See you tomorrow.*"

The line disconnected, and I frowned at the handset.

"He will be okay, Taylor," Harper said.

It seemed like he was continually reassuring me for some reason or another. I looked over at him and fell deep into his olive-green eyes. Those eyes were the same ones that I had fallen in love with, even in wolf form when we'd first interacted.

18

"I hope so," I sighed. "He doesn't seem much like himself."

"It's hard losing someone that you love."

I nodded. "I just wish that I could do more for him."

"You're doing enough just by being there. He knows where to find you if he needs more than that."

I ran my fingers over Harper's cheek. It was a little rough since he hadn't shaved in a couple of days.

His eyes watched me closely for a few measured seconds, and then his lips sank to mine. Want, need, hunger, lightning, everything ran through me. His hand cradled my neck as he moved over me to pin me beneath him. His fingers laced through mine, and I squeezed his hand tight, pushing it up, so I was on top of him. A few months ago, I would have been mortified at the thought of being in any way assertive when it came to being with any guy, but I suppose that love gives you confidence that you never knew.

I leant forward and drank him in, my hair hanging over him like chestnut-coloured curtains. His warm hands moved up my sides, sending a tremor through me.

And then, something changed. My breath seemed to all but disappear. I stopped and sat back, resting my hands on his chest. Harper's brows pinched, darkening the colour of his eyes.

"Taylor?" he said.

My hands moved to rest on my thighs, and the tightness in my chest pulled tighter. My nails sank into the flesh on my legs, and suddenly, I was gasping into a scream; a horrible wail that seemed to echo through the night. I felt Harper cringe from beneath me, and only half comprehended that the screech would pierce his already sensitive wolf-hearing.

I exhaled in a heap and felt my shoulders shaking. At first, I thought that I was having some kind of seizure, but then I felt the pressure of Harper's fingers around my upper arms.

"Taylor," he breathed. His voice was urgent. "Taylor, are you all right?"

I couldn't find my voice to reply that I was fine. Whatever feeling had come, had gone again with my breath.

"You shouldn't be here," another voice answered. "Do you have a death wish, Wolfie?"

I groaned internally and twisted to see Sal. Salvatore Vincent.

"What are you doing here, Grim?" Harper snarled.

Sal smirked. "I heard your girlfriend scream and came to avenge her."

"Shut up, Sal," I exhaled, twisting to my feet. I swayed a little, and Sal stepped forward. I brushed off his hand.

"Are you okay? What did you scream for?" he asked. "You've got around another twenty-one days until your next change, so—"

"I know, Salvatore," I sighed. "And I don't know. I… it was really weird."

Harper's arm moved around my shoulder, and I gripped his shirt.

Sal folded his arms. His orange-coloured eyes looked eerie in the darkness. They reminded me of the golden eyes of the flesh-eating wendigo that had stalked me after I'd gotten back from Italy a few months ago.

I shook my head. "I'm fine now though, so you can go, Sal."

"Me? Are you kidding? There's a wolf-hunter that works on campus, and you two are canoodling across the road in the bushes. Then you, Mistry, start screaming like a flipping banshee—"

"I am a banshee," I snapped. "Now get out of here before I give you something to scream about, Reaper."

"Kinky. But seriously. Get out of here. Theo lives in student accommodation, and Harper is no-doubt on his hit-list after you went and paraded him around in front of him a few days ago."

I scoffed. "It was hardly a parade."

Theo Asimi, the Greek wolf-hunter, was the administrative assistant that had made me a new student ID card after I'd lost my old one during exams. It was only upon meeting him then that I realised that I had met him before. I'd been out with him once after Harper first left for my safety. He also worked for the university information systems department in the library and had the same purple wolfsbane flower tattoo on his wrist that Leo Gatto, my Italian flame, had. Leo had told me that it was a family symbol. I guess I didn't know at the time that family to him ran deeper than blood.

"Whatever. Just go somewhere that's not so open and creepy," Sal mumbled.

"As if I'd let him hurt Harper, seriously, Sal—"

"Mistry," Sal near shouted. "I'm not being funny. Wolf-hunters know their stuff, and regardless of whether you can wail louder than anyone on earth, he will out-fight the both of you. Now quit being stubborn and, just for *once*, just do what I'm telling you to."

"Maybe the Grim is right," Harper murmured.

Sal exhaled. "Thank you, at least someone sees sense."

"Since when do you care about Harper's welfare, Sal?" I frowned.

"Since when do you not?"

I shook my head. "I wouldn't let anything happen to him."

"You." He huffed. "Do you really think that a wolf-hunter wouldn't have one of those fancy silver daggers to slice right through your heart? You'll be dead before you can even take a breath."

"And he'll be a banshee." I shrugged. "He wouldn't take that risk."

His head shook. "Wolf-hunters are protected by their mark… why must you argue with me *all the time?*"

Harper pulled me against him. "Come on, Taylor. We should go."

I frowned and leant over to pick up the emerald-coloured blanket that we'd been lying on, and then stormed passed Sal towards my silver four-wheel drive. I climbed in the driver's side and slammed the door, glowering at where Sal was still standing. He was talking to Harper, which usually made me nervous. Only this time, neither of them looked like they were wearing the usual snarl that they usually wore when they were together.

I considered holding down my hand on the car horn, but thought better of it. I'd already made enough noise tonight.

After a moment, Harper nodded and started to make his way over to me. I shuffled in my seat.

"What did he want?" I mumbled.

Harper looked up and smiled. "Would you like me to drive?"

"No, I can drive," I said, turning the key. "What did Sal say to you?"

"He is just concerned."

I huffed. "Sure he is, about himself."

"About you," Harper replied. His voice sounded weird, so I glanced at him. He was frowning.

"Why me?"

"Something happened to you before, Taylor. Don't you remember?"

I shrugged. "I got a bit breathless and screamed, it was nothing."

"Breathless?"

"A little. Like I said, it obviously passed since I had enough air to scream." I laughed.

Harper's frown deepened. "I'm not sure that it is a laughing matter. Perhaps we need to speak to Cole."

"Not tonight, Harper," I groaned. "Let's just go back to my place and put on a movie or something."

Harper's hand found mine, and he squeezed it. "Okay, tomorrow then. As long as you're feeling all right now."

"I feel great."

Worry was still hanging on his brow.

"Seriously, Harper. I feel fine. Promise."

He nodded but didn't look convinced. I suppose I would just have to convince him when I wasn't operating heavy machinery.

The unit was dark when we arrived home. Jesse must have forgotten to leave a light on when he dropped off his camping things. I went and grabbed a glass of water from the kitchen, and then headed over to the television.

"What do you want to watch?"

"I don't mind, Taylor, you pick." Harper smiled.

He sat down on the couch and my black cat, Raven, darted out from underneath, hissing as she ran towards my room.

My kitten had grown a lot since I'd found the timid animal under my car about four months ago. She had never liked Harper though. Maybe she knew that he turned into a giant dog once a month and had a healthy aversion to him. Harper had said that he'd never been a cat person, but I knew that he was lying. His closest and oldest friend was Hunter, and she was a part-time black panther. He'd also alluded once that they had shared more than a friendship between them, but I didn't like to dwell on that. I was insecure enough with her being his friend, never mind a former *girl*friend.

"Something wrong?" Harper asked.

I looked up and shook my head, then scrolled through Netflix until I found a movie to watch. Once I'd hit play, I nestled in beside him, and his arm moved around my shoulder.

"Harper?"

"Yes, Taylor?"

"I'm sorry about before," I said. "We were in the middle of something, and I went and ruined it."

I could feel myself blushing, and Harper moved to run his fingers down my cheek. They felt as warm as my flushed skin.

"You didn't ruin anything," he whispered.

I tipped my head up to kiss him, and he took a breath. His hand moved to my arm.

"What's wrong?" I frowned.

"Nothing."

"Harper—" I heard keys in the door and looked behind me towards the sound. "Who on earth—?"

The door opened, and I groaned.

"Hey, lovebirds, I didn't think that you'd be here," Brandon said.

"I live here," I replied. "What are you doing here?"

He shrugged. "This place is closer than my place."

"Closer to what? Weren't you out with Eden?"

He yawned. "Yup, that. What are you watching?"

He collapsed down beside me, and I pulled a face.

"Oh, I wanted to see this one. This is that Shailene Woodley film, right? She's a total fox, don't you think, Harper?"

Harper knitted his lips together. Smart.

I frowned. "Brandon, go home."

"What? Why?" he sighed and then began wiggling his eyebrows. "Oh, I get it."

I smacked him in the chest, and he doubled over. I didn't think I'd hit him that hard, but maybe since I was laced with silver now, it carried more weight. Ugh, weight.

"Fine then, I'll go." Brandon coughed. "There's no need for abuse, Tay."

I rolled my eyes. "Why didn't you go back and hang with Eden? Or did you two break-up again?"

"Nope, nothing like that." He shrugged. "She got a call, and just up and left."

I glanced at Harper who raised his eyebrows. Eden was a firefighter and a Shadow Weaver. Either could have been the cause of her abrupt departure.

"But I suppose I'll be going," Brandon sighed. "All the way home... on my own... alone... to be lonely."

My eyebrows lifted, but Harper nudged me. I looked at him, and he tipped his head. My eyes rolled.

"Fine, you can stay. Jesse said that he wouldn't be home tonight anyway," I grumbled. "You can stay in his room."

Brandon pulled a face. "Where is Jess? I thought that he was here?"

"No, he said that he was going out with someone, and not to expect him home. He didn't tell you?"

That concerned me. Brandon was his best friend, and he told him as much as he told me – or as little as he told me, as it were.

"Who was he going out with? Did he say?" Brandon asked.

I shrugged. "No, he didn't. I thought that you would know who it was."

"It's probably a chick."

"There is no way that it's a girl. He's still heartbroken over Ashley," I sighed. "He couldn't move on that fast."

"I'm not talking about moving on, I'm talking about having fun and forgetting about stuff," Brandon said. The way he said it made me blush.

26

I shook my head. "No, Jesse isn't like that."

"Tay, every guy is like that. Right, Harper?"

"Don't," I snapped. My finger lifted towards him and his eyebrows lifted innocently. I didn't need to hear, in so many words, that Harper had been with, and therefore needed to get over other girls. He had never told me just how many there had been, and a part of me was glad for that, but the other part only suspected the worst.

"Jesse is not like you, Brandon. He wouldn't do that," I said. I stood up and folded my arms, and saw Harper sigh.

"Then who is he out with, Taylor?" Brandon countered. "And why wouldn't he tell you or me about it? It's obviously because he's not proud of it… because you'd look at him all judgemental like the way you're looking now."

I gritted my teeth and clenched my fists.

"Enough," Harper said calmly. His hands were restraints on my shoulders. I could have easily shrugged them off, but I really didn't want to pummel Brandon. Even if he aggravated me now, I was sure that in the morning I would feel bad about it. Well, pretty sure.

"I'm getting tired, Taylor," Harper said. "Let's go to bed."

Brandon's eyebrows lifted smugly, and I wanted to smack them off his face. Harper turned me towards the corridor to my room.

"Go home, Brandon," I called.

"Goodnight, Taylor," he answered.

I went to turn to go back, but Harper grabbed my hand and reached to push open my door.

"Enough, Taylor," Harper whispered. "He is inconsequential."

"He's a jerk is what he is," I grumbled. "And I thought Sal was bad."

Harper huffed. "Oh, he is. They both are."

I smiled and instantly felt my mood lift. Harper's eyes glowed.

"Your heart is beating very fast, Taylor," he said.

"It only beats for you." I shrugged and then laughed. "Sorry, that was terrible."

He leant down and kissed my neck. "Don't apologise."

My eyes closed and my breathing felt tight again. It wasn't in the same way as it had felt before. This time it was in the way that it always seemed to get when Harper was close to me, kissing me, and touching me like he was now.

"Brandon is in the next room," I murmured.

Harper reached to push the door closed. "Please don't be thinking about Brandon right now, Taylor."

I breathed a laugh. "I—"

My words were cut off as his lips sank to mine. I thought that I heard a small growl from the back of his throat, and it made my stomach tighten. I may still have been a bit uneasy when it came to this sort of stuff, but I couldn't deny that I loved the effect that I seemed to have on Harper. It confounded me that I could drive him as crazy as he drove me.

He backed me onto my bed as his lips ran down my throat. I took the opportunity to catch my breath.

"Harper."

"Mm?"

There was a short pause as I tried to form the words that didn't want to come out. Harper pulled back to study my features.

"Okay, I'll stop," he whispered.

My head shook apologetically. We had been intimate before, but that was in a place that no one would ever think to be near enough to disturb us. The Amund Tomb, the place that resembled a sort of sanctity for me. I'd always found refuge and protection there, and the most vivid times seemed to be with Harper.

"I'm sorry, I—"

"You don't need to explain or apologise," he murmured. "I told you. Whatever you're comfortable with."

I shuffled up to reach my pillow and kicked off my shoes. Harper stepped back.

"You're staying though, right?" I said. "I don't want you to go."

He drew in a breath and nodded. "Okay."

I shimmied out of my jeans and kicked them to the floor as he sat on the bed. It wasn't until I'd tucked myself under the covers that he lay down beside me. I felt like I had ruined something between us. I know that he said that he was okay with me taking things at my own pace, but I couldn't help but feel like maybe he wasn't. I was too afraid to ask just in case I was right.

"Harper?"

"Mm?"

"You can come under the covers, I'll share," I said.

He turned his head to look at me, then smiled weakly. A second later, he was standing again, removing his shoes and jeans. He stepped towards the bed again.

I propped myself up on my elbows. "I know that you don't normally sleep in a T-shirt."

"Neither do you."

I looked down. "I know I keep changing the rules. I just don't want to make things harder for you."

"What's hard for me?"

I shrugged. "Us being together was a big step for me, and even if it was a-amazing, I still feel self-conscious sometimes."

Harper sat back down. "I know that you do, and I understand that."

"Do you?"

"Do you not think that I do?"

"No, I do." I nodded. "I mean, I know that you try, but I also know that I'm probably not like any of the other girls that you've been with."

"I don't expect you to be," he whispered. "I want to be with you because you're you."

I pressed my lips together. "Okay."

"All right?"

"Yes," I exhaled.

His hand brushed over my shoulder. "I love you, Taylor. Only you, for who you are. That's enough for me."

Sometimes I found it really difficult to understand how I could deserve someone like Harper. Then I remembered that affections weren't about being rewarded for anything, they just were.

"I love you too. So much that it's a little scary."

He reached under my pillow and pulled out the singlet that I usually slept in.

"Be comfortable," he said.

I nodded. "You too."

He chuckled. "We are a strange pair."

I smiled, and then lifted my hand to my chest, feeling the tightness again.

"Taylor?" Harper breathed. He walked around and knelt in front of me.

I clawed at my throat then tipped my head back, squeezing my neck as another scream forced its way out my body in a shrill cry of death. Harper clutched at his ears and dropped onto the floor. I half expected the windows to shatter, or Brandon to run in to see what was torturing me. A tear trickled down the side of my face as I caught my breath. I blinked down at Harper.

"Harper, Harper," I murmured. I sank onto the floor beside him.

Harper clutched my arms and then ran his hand over my neck and shoulders. "Are you all right?"

"I... yes, are you?"

"Me? Yes, I'm fine."

I looked around. "I don't know what's happening to me. I don't know why that happened."

He stood up and pulled me with him. "Come on, I'm taking you to Cole."

"Not now, please," I breathed. "I'm tired. Can we just go to sleep?"

Worry darkened his eyes again.

"Please, Harper, we'll see him first thing," I sighed. "I'm okay now. Honestly."

He frowned and I turned to change into my singlet, throwing my top and bra to the floor near my jeans. I climbed back in bed and waited while Harper removed his T-shirt and then slipped under the blankets, wrapping his arms around me.

It was enough.

*

Jesse still wasn't home when we got up, but Brandon was still fast asleep and making himself at home in my house. Harper and I left him and went out for breakfast at *Clair De Lune*, before heading over to Cole's apartment. Harper was still on a mission to try to make sense of my strange breathlessness and compulsion to scream the night before.

"Inhale, Taylor," Cole said, pressing the stethoscope to my back. I did as I was told. "And exhale."

I breathed out and sighed. "I feel fine now. It passed pretty quickly, both times."

Cole wrapped the stethoscope around his neck and folded his arms.

"It has to have something to do with what you are, but I don't understand it," Cole said. "I'm sorry, Taylor. I do not know much about banshees. You are the first that I have come across."

I stood up and pulled my cardigan back on. "It's okay, Cole. We're all in the same boat."

"But it has to mean something." Harper huffed. He was pacing, and it was making me nervous for no reason. "She felt breathless, she… she screamed, and it wasn't even a Full Moon. This can't affect her all the time, this banshee thing, can it?"

I didn't really understand what it meant before, but I was beginning to now. If I was going to be on the verge of transforming all month round, then it put Harper in some kind of danger. Silver was lethal to him, and it was embedded in me. Though, come my time to change into the white woman, that defence came to the surface.

"Harper, there's no reason why you should be worried," Cole said calmly. I admired his demeanour. He had obviously been a doctor for a long time and had to deal with worried loved-ones. "For all intents and purposes, Taylor seems perfectly healthy and normal."

"But she's not normal, Cole, she's supernatural," Harper barked. "Normal to a supernatural is not normal."

I looked up as Ruby appeared and smiled at her. She handed me a glass of water.

"I'm sorry," I whispered, though I knew that she could hear me clearly. "He's just worried about me."

Ruby smiled, and her silver eyes twinkled. "I know. We all are. But you seem to be handling it all well."

"As well as can be expected." I shrugged. "I've finally realised that there are some things that I can't control and trying to will only stress me out more."

"That's very wise." She nodded.

I drew in a breath, and it caught in my throat as a maroon pillar of smoke appeared between Ruby and I. It was Eden with her fancy Shadow Weaver method of travel.

I was about to roll my eyes at her but then realised that she didn't look like her usual sarcastic, holier-than-thou self.

"Eden, what's wrong?" Cole asked.

"I just wanted to come and say goodbye for a while," she said. Her hands ran through her short red hair. "Um, I need to be with my family, so I won't be around."

I looked at Harper, and he shared the same look of curiosity. Eden had gotten a call last night and left Brandon to harass us... why?

"What happened, Eden?" Ruby asked. "Is everything okay?"

Eden exhaled in a groan. "No, Joel's fiancée died last night. She was the Light Lacer who was pregnant."

Ruby's pale hand lifted to her mouth. "Oh gosh, I'm so sorry. Is... did the baby survive?"

Eden nodded. "She did, but Joel made the Lacers take her to their reservation. The Weavers that were circling are pretty interested in a quarter-caste."

"Quarter-caste?" I frowned. "Do you mean the baby is only a quarter Weaver?"

"Yes, Joel is Eden's foster brother, he is half-Weaver, half-Lacer," Cole replied. "Remember that Rob mentioned that he had some success healing his full-Lacer mate once, considering their compatibility?"

I blinked. "Sort of."

"It was when Harper was… recovering from the banshee attack," Ruby added.

"Oh, well naturally I block out a lot of those memories." I answered. "I suppose as vampires though, your memories are pretty crisp."

"Anyway, Joel is understandably pretty cut up and needs us," Eden said. "You'll understand if—"

"What about Brandon?" I asked. "Have you spoken to him?"

Eden frowned. "No, he's just a boy. My family is more important."

"You should tell him, Eden. You can't just disappear."

She scoffed, instantly reminding me of the Eden that I knew and, well, just knew.

"Well, you can tell him then," she snapped. "I'm sure that he'll enjoy crying on your shoulder, Taylor."

I recoiled. "I don't know what that's supposed to mean, but—"

"Please." She huffed.

Eden and I had our ups and downs, but we were getting along better after we opened up the lines of communication and put aside our differences – her obnoxiousness and my alleged selfishness. We still had our moments though. Apparently, this was one of them.

"Eden, what time did the Lacer die?" Harper asked. "You said that it was night?"

Her expression instantly softened. "I don't know. Joel didn't go into specifics."

"You don't think…?" Cole frowned in thought.

"Maybe, possibly…" Harper mumbled. "One of the times…"

"What?" Ruby asked before I could get the word out. I was still a little miffed at Eden's insinuation that Brandon wanted me to be there for him.

Cole and Harper looked at me, and their silver eyes and green eyes prickled my skin.

"What? It wasn't me!" I gasped. "I was with Harper all night."

"Not you, per se," Cole said. "But you did scream, perhaps—"

"Maybe you felt her death," Harper finished. "It makes sense. It would be the only thing that explains it."

Eden's expression was a mixture of anger and confusion. Or maybe the anger was fuelled by confusion.

"What about the banshee?" Eden asked. "Did she do something else?"

"No, she just… last night she got a little breathless and let out one of her—"

"Death cries?" Eden finished. "Are you sure? Maybe she just broke a nail."

I frowned at my cuticles. "I don't really have long nails."

Eden scoffed. "This is ridiculous. I just wanted to say bye, so… bye."

She turned her head and erupted into smoke. The two vampires and Harper exchanged curious glances. Though, Cole's expression was a little more thoughtful.

Ruby looked at me a little apologetically. "I'm sure she's just upset for her foster brother."

"She's never really warmed to me," I sighed.

Harper looked back at Cole.

"Do you think that it could be possible?" he asked. "Do you think that Taylor still feels supernatural deaths, even if she doesn't participate in them?"

Cole shrugged. "It could be true, it's highly possible. When I was talking to Sal about reaping humans, he mentioned feeling something, although human reaping is more tactile."

"But didn't Joel and the twins live up in the hills? That's miles away, Cole," Ruby added.

"That's true, but we are dealing with the supernatural, there are no limits," Cole replied. "For all we know, banshees could be like the supernatural anchor for the souls to pass through to find peace in the afterlife. My knowledge of banshees is limited to Taylor. Perhaps Salvatore will know more."

"The Grim knows nothing," Harper mumbled. "He will be no help."

"Regardless, he could shed some light on the new information that we have been given."

"Possible information," I said.

The three sets of eyes turned to look at me. I'd been somewhat of a piece of misplaced furniture while they deliberated my fate.

"It all seems a little—" Ruby started, but was interrupted when a grey burst of smoke filled the room, followed by Eden's maroon one, and then an orange, and a red. Suddenly Cole's lounge room was very crowded.

"Joel, Xavier, Raphael," Cole said. He reached his hand towards the additions. The two identical boys shook it, but the other one just looked around the room. His eyes were blood-shocked, not in a substance abuse way, but in a haven't-slept-been-crying-all-night kind of way. I deduced that this was Joel.

"Where is she?" he asked. "The one who felt Luna die."

Harper edged towards me, and I straightened. Ruby took a measured step towards me too, but somehow, I thought that if the light-and-shadow magic hybrid wanted to hurt me, I'd be smoke. Literally.

"Hi," I murmured. "My name is Taylor. I'm sorry for your loss."

He stared at me with grey eyes that were a flat and eerie version of the silver vampire colour that I was used to seeing. I swallowed.

"You're the banshee?" he asked.

I forced myself to nod.

"Eden said you screamed for her, for Luna," Joel said. His voice broke on her name. He was a man in flames but staying alive. He would live forever covered in them. As a half-Weaver, half-Lacer, literally nothing could kill him. He could heal from everything. He was indestructible. He was suffering.

"I felt something," I replied. "I felt breathless, and as if the air had been sucked away from me. I felt the void, and I had to scream. I had to, but I didn't know why. It could have been for her."

Joel was nodding, and his eyes were swimming. They were red rock pools, thrashing with pain, and eternal youth. He didn't look older than twenty. My heart broke for him.

"She was too weak, she was too broken, I couldn't heal her," he barely breathed. I struggled to hear him, but I was the furthest away without super-hearing. One of the twins, the one wearing red, rested a comforting hand on his shoulder and he shattered, sinking to the floor with the weight of the world.

I didn't know what I was doing. I was never really good with tears. They scared me because they were raw emotion that I tried to bury. Emotion was dangerous, it made you vulnerable. Regardless, I found myself walking over to him – to the broken man on the floor. The red twin beside him glared at me.

"It's okay, Raph, she won't hurt him," Cole said.

The red twin, Raphael, stepped behind Joel, like some kind of fireball bodyguard. He reminded me a little of Eden. I suppose hot-bloodedness ran in the family.

I pressed my lips together and dropped to my knees in front of Joel, hesitating before resting my hands on his shoulders. He flinched at my touch, but then looked up and frowned at me. He blinked a few times.

"I can feel it in you, the silver," he murmured. "You're strong."

My hands lifted and he reached to grasp them. One of them felt hot, the other iced cold. I didn't know whether to sweat or shiver.

"I can feel it in you too, it's—" I gasped as a glimmer of silver light seemed to fringe his form. "Don't... don't give up. It's not the end, you can't give up. You have to think of your daughter."

"What is she muttering about?" Eden snapped.

Joel seemed to pale. "I can't... I can't do this without her. We... we were supposed to do it together."

Suddenly I was blinking back tears. "She needs you now, they both need you. You need to stay strong. You are strong – stronger than you seem, stronger than you feel. Joel, you need to live."

"This is ridic—"

"Quiet, Eden," the orange twin snapped. Xavier, I assumed, he seemed to be the reasonable one of the three of them. Eden had mentioned once that he was logical and more level-headed when she had told me about her brothers.

Joel squeezed my hands tighter, but I didn't feel discomfort in the grasp. I did feel the heat and cold, but I knew that it was nothing compared to what Joel must be feeling inside, so I fought through it. My feelings were insignificant.

Joel didn't speak words, but I could see in his eyes that he had given up. I stared back at him, trying to give him some of my strength, some of any of the hope that I felt for him, for life, for living, for *love*. He looked down, and I watched as the light around him began to dim a little. His eyes lifted, and they weren't alive, but they had life in them again, which was more than before.

"Taylor," he sighed.

I nodded. Any words that I said would only fail.

"Thank you," he finished.

I exhaled. "You're welcome."

Joel's grip loosened, and I sank back to my heels as he stood. He sniffled, wiping his face on the elbow of his shirt, and then took a breath.

"I… I'm sorry for intruding. Forgive me," he said.

"It's never an intrusion, Joel," Cole replied.

The dark-haired, half-caste nodded at Cole and then gave one final nod at me before bursting into grey smoke. Raphael and Xavier exchanged a look, and then Raphael left in a red puff. Eden didn't bother with another goodbye, but just disappeared in her maroon pillar of smoke. I looked up at the final Weaver standing above me as he lowered to kneel.

"Taylor, my name is Xavier Marrone," he said. "I don't know what you just did for my brother, but thank you. He needed reminding that there is life after death, and I don't think anyone else could have helped him the way that you did."

I shook my head. "I still don't know exactly what I did."

"You gave him hope."

I swallowed, and Xavier stood.

"I'm sorry, Cole. I'm sorry that we couldn't meet again under better circumstances," Xavier said.

"Please pass on my good wishes to Rob and Ebony," Cole replied. "Our thoughts are with your family at this difficult time."

"Thank you." Xavier nodded. Then a twirl of orange smoke filled the air.

Harper was over to me in what felt like less than a second. I wondered how hard it was for him to stand by during the whole ordeal.

"Are you okay, Taylor?" Harper asked. "Did he hurt you?"

"No," I answered. "He's just hurt."

Harper reached for my hands and then flinched, muttering something quick in French that I missed.

I looked down at them and noticed that one was red and one was white. I pressed them together and they sizzled with steam.

"Silver," I murmured. "I guess I'm more of a conductor than I realised."

"Yes," Cole answered. "But a conductor for what, exactly?"

I frowned up at him. "What do you mean?"

"I mean, I think you did something more than give Joel encouraging words," he replied. "I wish that I knew more about your kind."

My kind.

It was the first time that anyone had ever stated that I was different, that I had a kind that wasn't like any other that we knew. A part of me felt like I belonged somewhere, but I didn't know where, so I didn't feel entirely comforted by it. I felt lonelier than ever.

"Come on," Harper said. "Let me take you home."

I let Harper help me stand and nodded.

"Jesse should be home," I replied.

Facing Jesse, even though the loss of his love had been over a week ago, would be harder than anything that I had faced with Joel. I didn't know how to help my twin brother. What's worse, I didn't even know if he wanted my help.

*

"He's asleep," Brandon said as I stepped through the door. I groaned and threw my keys at the table. They slid along the wood and fell onto the floor, making Raven jump and dart around into Brandon's lap. Somehow, that made me more annoyed.

"Why are you still here, Brandon?" I asked.

"I'm going soon," he sighed. "I'm just waiting to hear back from Eden."

Eden.

Crap.

"I, um," I looked back at Harper who pressed his lips together. Double crap. I was apparently on my own on this one. Why did I always have to break up with guys that I was never dating?

"Listen, Brandon," I started. "We need to talk."

Harper shook his head. Was that wrong to start with?

"I mean, I need to tell you something," I amended.

Brandon turned. "What's up? Did something happen? Did you hit my car?"

The stupid silver ute.

"No, rest assured that your car is just as useless and intact as you left it," I answered. "It's actually about Eden."

Harper frowned. Apparently, I was worse at this than I thought.

"What about her?" Brandon asked. "Did you see her? Is she okay?"

I scratched my head. "She, well, her, um..."

Brandon groaned. "Cough it up, Taylor."

"She had to go away for a while. Her family is going through some stuff, and she said to say that she won't be around, and goodbye, I guess."

43

"What?" Brandon blinked.

I shrugged. "Sorry."

"You're kidding, right? Is this your version of a joke? Are you just trying to get rid of me?"

I heard Harper exhale. Maybe my attempt at complete honesty had its drawbacks. It just sounded like I was being the usual petulant self that I became whenever I was around Brandon.

"No, not a joke," I answered. "She's gone, Brandon. She won't be around any more."

"Why would she tell you that? She doesn't even like you."

I pouted. "She doesn't?"

"You're surprised?"

"I guess not," I sighed. "But to be honest, she wasn't going to even tell you. I was the one who thought that you should know."

Harper rubbed his shaking head.

Brandon frowned. "What is your problem? Why do you have to be so mean?"

"I'm not mean, I'm just saying that she is the one who didn't have the guts to tell you herself," I replied. "At least I'm honest with you."

"There's honest, and then there's cruel. That was just uncalled for." Brandon huffed and stood up, heading towards the kitchen.

I looked over at Harper and lifted my hands. "What did I say?"

Harper's mouth opened, but his words were cut off by another voice.

"What is all the shouting about?" Jesse croaked. "Can't a guy get some sleep in his own house?"

"Jesse," I sighed. "You're here."

"Oh, you know," Brandon answered. "Your sister just broke up with me for Eden. Nothing serious."

I rolled my eyes. "You are so dramatic."

"Well, that's what you're doing, isn't it? Served with a side of *I told you so*."

Jesse cringed at the volume. "Can you two just shut up or go somewhere else?"

I looked over at my brother. He hardly ever got infuriated with Brandon or me. I noticed that his eyes looked red, but it was a different red to the upset way that Joel's had been – they looked red and glassy because of substance influence.

"Are you hung-over?" I asked. "When did you get home?"

"Don't know." He shrugged. "It's really none of your business though."

I glanced at Brandon who looked equally as confused at Jesse's attitude. It was entirely unlike him.

"How did you get home?" I frowned.

Jesse yawned. "You're not my carer, Taylor. Back off."

"Hey, she's only worried," Brandon said. "We both are."

Jesse laughed, but it sounded flat. "So now you agree with each other. Perfect, I'm going back to bed."

"Jess—" I started. Harper caught my wrist, and I pivoted.

"Leave him be," Harper murmured. "He needs his own space."

Jesse looked up and nodded at Harper, then disappeared behind the wall of the corridor. A moment later, I heard his door close.

I frowned at Harper. "What was that?"

"He's grieving, Taylor, just give him time."

"He needs his family and friends around him. He needs to know that we're here for him."

"He knows that you're here," Harper answered. "But people grieve in different ways. Some prefer to be—"

"A lone wolf?"

His shoulders dropped. "I don't want to fight with you. Please don't turn this into an argument."

I exhaled and ran my hands through my hair. "I'm not, I'm just worried. He's never been like this before; he's always been able to talk to me about everything, but this time he's just closing himself off. I don't understand it."

"I know, me neither," Brandon replied.

I hadn't been talking to him, but naturally, he had invited himself into business that wasn't his.

"I think I'm just going to go for a run, I need to clear my head," I sighed. I hadn't been for a run in a while, but I'd always found a kind of calmness in nature.

Harper stepped back. "You want to be alone."

"I'll call you later."

I turned and headed towards my room.

"Looks like it's just you and me," Brandon said. "They're more alike than they realise."

"Goodbye, Brandon," Harper replied.

I heard the front door open and close and hoped that meant that it wasn't just Harper who had left. I didn't want to talk to Brandon.

When I had changed, I walked back out. Brandon was leaning on his knees as Raven circled his ankles. He didn't look up.

I sighed. "You okay?"

He didn't answer.

"Brandon?"

Nothing.

I walked over and sat beside him. He still didn't look up.

"Her family is going through some pretty heavy stuff," I murmured. "Someone close to them died, so they're pulling together. It's not you; she just needs to be with them right now."

"You don't have to make me feel better," he grumbled.

"I know. But it's the truth."

He looked up. "Did she really have no intention of telling me?"

"I don't think it's that she didn't want to tell you, I think it was more that she couldn't tell you," I said. "I think she didn't want to let you down, and she couldn't deal with more sadness in her life than she's already facing."

Brandon smiled weakly. "Thank you."

"For what?"

"For lying to me," he whispered. "That's probably the nicest thing that you've ever done for me."

I rolled my eyes. It could have been true.

He rested a hand on my wrist. I looked down at it and wondered if moving my hand away would offend him.

"What are we going to do about Jesse?" he asked.

"Nothing. Maybe Harper is right. Maybe he just needs space to wrap his head around it all."

Brandon dropped his hand, and I exhaled.

"It's just not like him," he said. "He's not acting like himself."

"I don't know what else to do." I shrugged. "Everything I say to him just pushes him further away. Maybe the thing to do is just be here for him until he's ready to come to me."

"We all lost Ashley though."

"Not in the same way."

"I know, but it's not healthy what he's doing."

I shook my head. "But who are we to judge what is best for him? I hate it, but I understand his need to try and find his bearings in his own way."

Brandon wrapped his arm around my shoulder, and I froze.

"He's just got you and me now," he said. "We have to stick together."

I stood up to escape his embrace. It made me uncomfortable.

Brandon blinked. "Tay? You all right?"

"I... I need to go for a run."

He nodded. "Okay, I'll see you when you get back."

I sighed and turned towards the door.

"Hey, Brandon?"

"Yes, Taylor?"

"Jesse has more than just you and me," I replied. "He has lots of friends and family who are here from him. He's not alone, none of us is. He'll see that when he wants to, and he'll be surrounded by people who love and support him."

Brandon frowned. "Okay."

I pressed my lips together and reached for the door handle.

"And Brandon?" I added. "There is no you and me."

He huffed a humourless laugh. "Got it. Loud and clear."

I smiled weakly and slipped out the door. I started running before it had even swung closed.

I didn't stop, even when I felt like I might collapse, I pushed through it. I needed to. I was out of shape, and it bothered me. So I kept running for as long as I could. Maybe it was half an hour, maybe more.

As I rounded back towards my block of units, I saw a dark shape leaning against a glinting black and chrome bike. I might have been exhausted, but seeing it only made me run faster.

Harper straightened as I got closer and I ran straight into his waiting arms. He groaned lightly at the force I hit him with.

"I'm sorry, I did leave, but I came back," he murmured. "I don't want to come between you and your brother."

"I think that I'm getting fat," I mumbled.

Harper breathed a laugh and pulled back to look at me. "What?"

"I'm so unfit. I think I'm putting on weight. I'm out of shape."

His hand brushed my cheek. "You're perfect."

I smiled but didn't believe him. Then something strange happened. It was something that I didn't expect to see again, but maybe my eyes were playing tricks on me. There was a flicker, a glimmer, a flash so quickly that a blink would have meant that I missed it. But I didn't. I saw Harper's light return and then dim. My mouth fell open, and I frowned.

"Did I say something wrong?" he asked.

So much had happened since he'd last spoken that I was confused by his question. I shook my head numbly and waited. Then, sure enough, it happened again. Like a neon light being switched on, it flickered again, once, twice, and then was a low glow that didn't disappear.

"Harper," I breathed. "I—"

"What?" he sighed. "What is it?"

I didn't know whether to tell him because I knew that it would come as a shock. But then, I didn't want to keep things from him either. I rubbed my eyes.

"I think that we need to see Cole," I said. "Maybe get him to rerun your bloodwork."

His head shook. "Why? What…? Oh. You see it again, the glow. It's returned."

"It started as a flicker, but it's turned back into a solid light," I replied. "It's not as bright as I've seen before though, not like Hunter or André's were."

I stopped and frowned. Harper reached around for his helmet and handed it to me. It amused me a little that he still insisted that I wore it when I was more durable than he was now.

He nodded. "Then let's go and see Cole."

Phase Two
The Mortal Wolf

It had only been two hours or so since we were last at the vampire's apartment, but everything looked and felt much different from the way we had left it.

Ruby wasn't there. She had gone to check on *Crescent*, the pub that Cole owned and she managed, near uni. I was a little bummed not to have the chance to talk to her about everything that had been happening lately. Ruby and I had become quite good friends since the whole marked-with-death thing, and other than Harper, Jesse, and maybe Sal; she was probably my only friend. She was definitely my only *female* friend. My former friend, April McKenzie, didn't even acknowledge me when I saw her around campus any more. Hunter had never warmed to me, and neither had Eden. I would like to say that I'd gotten along with Ashley when she was around, but we'd only really started being civil to each other in the weeks leading up to her death. I regretted that sometimes. A lot of the time. Once we'd finally got to talk about the rift between us, it turned out to be all one big misunderstanding. I'd like to say that my inability to make female friends was all due to a misunderstanding but, apparently, I was just a bit socially impeded.

"It's quite perplexing," Cole said. "I'll have to get it tested, but—"

"Is it possible that he's changed back into a mortal?" I asked. "I mean, it's not possible, is it? His body still heals. He heals himself, so his cells are in constant regeneration."

Harper walked over to stand beside me.

"It's hard to say, Taylor," Cole answered. "But we never did a blood screening after the… after he healed himself from the silver dagger, so perhaps he was never immortal. As I said at the time, it was only a concept that—"

"No," I sighed. "He… he can't be normal. He… if he can die, then that means that I could kill him."

Harper ran his hands up my arms. "It's okay, Taylor—"

"No, it's not, Harper. Don't you see what this means? You can die. If you glow, then come the Full Moon, I could take you away from this planet, and I can't lose you. I can't. There has been enough death lately without—"

"Taylor, that's not going to happen," Harper replied. "I'm not going anywhere."

I pouted. "You don't know that for sure."

"Do we know anything for sure? Except for the fact that I love you and I trust you."

"Harper," I whispered. "Don't… don't pretend like this isn't upsetting to you too."

"No matter how I feel about the situation, it doesn't change anything. You and I are still together, we are still strong, and I still will not let anything get in the way of that."

I bit my lip and nodded. Cole, who had been standing quietly through my entire bleak rant, lifted his pale hand to run through his blond hair. It was a bit curlier today than I was used to seeing it. The longer front bits were swept across his forehead and were tucked behind his ear.

"Taylor, I will get this tested as promptly as possible," Cole said quietly. "But I assure you that if Harper's blood still has werewolf healing qualities rather than any shifter-like qualities, then as Harper said, nothing has to change. You said that his glow wasn't bright, so that is promising—"

"But that can change in a split second," I interrupted. I seemed to be doing a lot of that today.

"Regardless, it's the best that we can hope for given the alternative."

I exhaled. "You're right. Sorry. I'm just... I'm scared."

"I understand. You have been through a lot lately, and knowing that there is more than a wolf-hunter out there that poses as a threat—"

"Oh my gosh – Theo," I sighed. "I completely forgot about him. What are we going to do?"

"I don't know," Harper answered. "He hasn't tried anything yet."

I frowned. "But we're not just going to wait around for him to try something, are we?"

"Taylor, please try to relax. Your heart is beating very fast."

"How am I supposed to relax when your life is in danger?"

"Harper is not in any direct harm," Cole said. "And he is welcome to stay here if it will make him feel safer. This goes without saying, but you are both always welcome here. Several floors are vacant where you can make yourself at home."

When he wasn't staying at my place, which admittedly was a lot, Harper had moved back into the cabin near the Stanley Colvin State Park that Hunter occupied when she was in South Coast. No one had seen her since the André incident, and I was relieved for the fact. I knew that if, and when, she did return that she'd have a bone to pick with me, despite the fact I had no control over his reaping.

I turned to Harper. "Please stay. I'll feel better if you stayed here."

"I... okay, but I doubt that there are any furnishings, and I can't move anything on my bike."

"I'll ask to borrow Brandon's ute. We can move things from the cabin."

"That's not necessary," Cole said. "Please just tell me what you need, and I can arrange it speedily."

"I can't ask you for that."

Cole smiled. "Please, friend, I'm offering."

It was funny to think that the most generous person that I knew was a vampire. It never ceased to amaze me that Cole was such a kind soul when arguably, vampires were soulless monsters. Arguably.

"Thank you." Harper nodded. "I cannot count the times that you have come to my assistance."

"There is no need to keep a tally. It's no trouble. You would do the same for me if the situation were reversed."

British chivalry.

"Thank you, Cole," I said. "And thank you for rerunning the blood."

Cole nodded. "I'll notify you immediately when I receive the results."

*

The next morning was Monday morning, and I was still knee-deep in winter term at uni to make up the credit for the one unit that I'd failed last semester. To be fair though, I was dealing with the news that I would turn into a screaming white woman and need to kill a supernatural creature at the next Full Moon. Given the circumstances, I think that only scoring low on one exam was better than failing all of them.

I made my own way to uni, determined to keep Harper as far from the campus as possible while we were still deciding what to do about Theo. After class, I headed to the library to find some books for secondary reading. I was only just thinking about how Theo had mentioned that he worked there when…

"Taylor Mistry," his voice said. It managed to make me shiver as I turned towards him.

"Theo Asimi."

"Still got that identity intact?" he asked.

I lifted the card that he'd made me between my fingers and he smiled.

"Excellent." He nodded. "Can't have you losing yourself."

"Oh, it's not that bad," I sighed. "I always either turn up or find some kind of replacement."

He chuckled. "Bit of light reading?"

I glanced down at the pile of books in my arms and tried to shrug.

"Winter term?" he pressed.

"The fun never stops."

He grinned. "I bet it's never a dull moment for you."

I felt my brows pinch and looked away from him. I don't know what he was insinuating, but I had a feeling that if I stood there any longer, then the conversation would take a turn in a direction that I wasn't prepared for.

"Well, I'd better get... go and do some... study," I stuttered. I took a step and nearly dropped my pile. Theo's arm shot out to stop the books from falling, and the purple wolfsbane tattoo on his wrist glared at me.

"Let me help you with those," he said.

"No, I've got them."

"Are you sure?"

I juggled the books into a more comfortable position. "Yes, positive. Uh, thanks."

Theo smiled again and took a step back. I hurried off to find a table that was far away from the technical support desk, but not too far that I was on my own. I would have otherwise left with the books, but there were a couple that weren't for loan. Got to love the closed reserve collection.

I turned a corner and walked right into someone else. My perfectly balanced books tumbled to the floor. Luckily, I was quick enough to jump back in time, as to not have them land on my feet. The person I had walked into wasn't so lucky. In fact, he began saying some choice expletives in Italian.

I groaned. It was Sal.

"Bloody hell, Taylor Mistry, I thought your bad luck had expired," he grumbled.

I shrugged. "It did. I wasn't the one who got pummelled with literature."

He rolled his orange eyes and began stacking them. I sank to my knees to help, considering they were my books.

Once they were all in a neat pile, Sal picked up the student card that I'd dropped.

"Don't want to lose this again." Sal chuckled.

I reached for it, and he pulled it back to look at.

"Are you serious?" He huffed, and his eyebrow rose.

I frowned. "What?"

"Taylor *Maye* Mistry."

"What about it?"

"Tailor made mystery," he laughed. "That's *gold*."

"Shut up." I muttered, snatching the card from him and smacking him with it.

"Ouch, hey," he groaned. "Haven't you harmed me enough with the book avalanche?"

I rolled my eyes and picked them up, straightening to stand.

"You walked into me. I was just trying to find a table—"

"What are you even doing here? You do know that Theo is here, right?" Sal whispered.

I sighed. "Yes, we were just having a chat."

"Having a chat? Are you mental?"

"Yes, I mean no. I'm not mental."

I began walking away; hoping that Sal would take the hint. He didn't.

"Well, I hope that Wolfie doesn't decide to make a surprise visit," he said, following me. "That won't end well."

"He's not going to. He's busy furnishing his new apartment."

"Apartment? Where? Is that safe?"

I stopped by a table and dropped everything on it. "Your concern for my boyfriend is a little concerning. Should I be worried?"

"Yes," Sal said earnestly. "You should be worried. There is a *wolf*-hunter in town, and your boyfriend just happens to be a—"

"Shh! For goodness sake, Salvatore, just go and broadcast that why don't you?"

"Well, those who matter know about the fact." He shrugged. "So where is he moving?"

I exhaled as he sat down opposite me. "Cole has some levels free in his building, so he's moving in there."

Sal nodded. "What safer place than in a bloodsucker's building?"

"Don't you have somewhere else to be that's nowhere near here?" I asked. "I mean, business can't be *that* quiet."

"Taylor Maye Mistry, you're not hoping that someone will die, are you?" he gasped in mock horror.

I shrugged. "Only someone who is suffering."

"If you want me to leave, all you have to do is—"

"Sal. Salvatore Vincent, please leave me alone."

Sal frowned. "Well, you don't need to be rude."

I sighed. I'd heard that a lot lately too. "Look, I just really can't afford to fail another unit."

He nodded. "I just don't like the thought of you being here alone when that wolf-hunter guy is here."

"It's not me that he's after. Besides, he wouldn't try anything in public."

"I just don't want to give him a chance. You've been through—"

"Enough, Sal. I'll be fine. Really," I replied. "I appreciate your concern, but I really think that it's misplaced."

He sighed and stood. "Okay, I get it. You don't need me any more."

"Sal, are you being pathetic?"

He smirked. "Maybe a little."

I rolled my eyes. "A lot."

"We used to hang out more."

"No, you used to actively try to avoid me more," I said. "But we can still hang out, I guess. We can trade stories."

"Cool." He nodded. "Hey, speaking of, did you find out what that screaming thing was about Saturday night?"

I bit my lip and glanced around to make sure that no one was in earshot. Sal stepped closer and leant towards me.

"I think, I *think* it was because a Lacer died," I whispered. "I think I sort of marked her death, or felt it, or something. It was weird."

Sal frowned. "That makes sense. It's weird that you were nowhere near her though."

"I know. Well, if that's what it was."

"What else would it be?" he asked. "How'd you come to that conclusion anyway?"

I drew in a breath. "Eden mentioned that her foster-brother-slash-half-Weaver-half-Lacer's fiancée died, so she'd be having family time for a while. He's taking it pretty hard.

Actually, the weirdest thing happened when I made contact with him."

"Wow, wow, wow," Sal said, sliding into the seat beside me. "When did you meet him?"

"Well, when she told us about it, Harper asked what time the Lacer had, you know, died, then she went all *Taylor is a weirdo* and left. The next minute she comes back with Joel and her twin Weaver brothers, and Joel's a complete mess, so I went over to him. It was so strange. Like I could feel his life energy or something. I could feel that he was giving up, and then he started to glow, like, really bright, and then something else happened, and it all kind of lifted. Like the cloud around him lifted and he was more, I don't know, hopeful or something."

Sal sat back with a look of confusion on his face. "Lifted? Like you healed his desire to die?"

"I don't know what it was." I shrugged. "I don't know what I did, but I did it, and he stopped glowing as bright."

Sal folded his arms, lifting his thumb to his lips. "That is strange."

"Did Alba ever mention anything about healing people or weird things like that?" I asked.

Alba had been the banshee that Sal had known before me. She's told him a couple of things about banshees but hadn't gone into the kind of great detail that I'd hoped for. Given the fact that she was no longer around, Sal thinks she was the banshee that I had replaced by stabbing her with the silver hunter's dagger. I hadn't intended to kill her at the time. I just was trying to stop her from *killing me*.

"No, she didn't talk much about her extracurricular activities. We reapers barely like to think about what we do," he murmured.

"Well, at least you don't trivialise it," I said. "At least death still means something to you."

"Without death, you don't get to experience life to the fullest," he replied. "It's easy to forget that, even if your days are numbered, you can still make them count. I like to think of the reaping as a reminder to make them count."

I smiled. "That's a really good way to look at it."

"The other way will kill you," he sighed, then stood up. "Or at least turn you into a cot-case."

"I guess so."

"Well, I should leave you to it," he said. "Taylor Maye Mistry, it's always a pleasure."

I rolled my eyes. "I'll see you, Sal."

"Don't you threaten me." He chuckled.

I threw my hand in his direction but, given he was several steps away, it was more of a figurative slap than an actual one. I watched as he made his way to the automatic glass door then sighed, looking around the library before me. My eyes wandered restlessly. I didn't want to be here, I felt like I had a million other more important things to do today rather than study up on something that I should have already learnt. It was hugely frustrating.

I looked back over towards the door as two noisy girls entered, and then nearly choked when behind them, Harper appeared.

Please let me be hallucinating.

Please.

He smiled when he saw me and made his way over. My head frantically thrashed around to make sure that Theo hadn't seen him. Maybe if he left now, then he could go without being noticed.

"Still here?" Harper sighed.

"What are you doing here? Theo is here," I whispered in a very useless loud whisper. I really just sounded like Batman.

Harper frowned. "Where? Why are you still here then?"

"Because he's not after *me*."

"We need to go."

"*You* need to go," I amended. "Harper, I need to study."

"Bring the books with you, hire them out."

"Some aren't for loan."

His head shook. "Then make copies of the pages that you need of them, and hire out the rest."

Huh, I never thought of that.

"Fine, I... I'll do it, just please wait outside," I said. "I really don't want him to see you."

I gathered my half-library of books and headed into the copy room. It was a smallish room, with no windows, and a creaky wooden door. Most of South Coast University was heritage listed, but I still didn't know why that meant they couldn't restore some of the parts that were falling apart. I left the door wide open and headed to the closest photocopier. There were two books that I needed to copy and at least a chapter in each of them. It would probably cost me a pile of money to get the pages that I needed, but if it meant that I would spend less time away from Harper, and less with Theo, then I would pay whatever I needed to.

I had nearly finished copying the pages in one of the books when I heard someone come in behind me.

"What are you?" the voice said.

I felt my shoulders tighten with stress and turned to see Theo at the door. He backed up against it to closed it and kicked a wedge beneath it. I swallowed.

"What are you doing, Theo?" I asked.

"I want to know what you are."

I breathed a flat laugh. "I'm a person. I'm a girl. What is your problem?"

He stepped forward, and for the first time, I saw that his hands were full. He was holding a bottle in one and something shiny and pointy in the other. A knife.

"Theo, are you crazy? What are you doing?" I frowned.

"I've seen you with the wolf," he said. "And I know they tend to travel in packs. I don't think that you're one of them, but I know that you're something. I want to know what you are."

"I'm nothing. I'm just a girl."

"Taylor, don't lie to me," he replied calmly.

My head shook. "I'm not lying."

I stepped away from the photocopier into the middle of the room. I didn't know what he was going to try, but I didn't want to be trapped between him and the machine.

"Fine." He nodded. "Be that way."

I could feel the scream sitting on my chest and tried to push it back. I knew that Harper would hear it and come to my rescue, and I couldn't risk him being here with Theo when he was armed. But what about me? What about that knife? What was that other substance that he held?

Theo thrust his hand forward, the one holding the bottle, and a second later, I felt the coldness of the liquid hit my skin. I don't know what I expected, but I didn't expect it to be what it was: colloidal silver.

I felt my skin absorb it. I felt the silver strengthen me. I swallowed the scream further down. Nothing supernatural was going to die right here and now. Perhaps someone human would though.

Theo's tanned skin seemed to pale as I stepped forward, clutching his neck just below his jaw with my hand. I felt my nails sink into his skin and wondered fleetingly when they had grown. I'd always kept them short.

"What... what—?" he gasped.

One of his hands raised to mine, but the other, oh the other, pushed the knife in it into my side. I gritted my teeth through the momentary pain, but again, felt strength from the silver. It mustn't have been a spelled knife like the one that Leo had. This one was just plain Ag.

I clutched him harder and lifted him up. He struggled, but it was all very silent. In fact, all I could hear was static. It was calm, with the slight rasping of breath that fought its way up Theo's closing neck. Then I heard another voice. The door hadn't opened, so that could only mean one thing.

"Taylor, stop," Sal whispered. "You're killing him."

I exhaled. "He started it."

"He's human."

"He's a hunter."

Sal's hand rested on my wrist, and I felt a surge of breathlessness that I guessed was something like what Theo was experiencing. My grip weakened and, eventually, I willed my fingers to straighten. Theo sank to the floor.

Sal frowned. "You're hurt."

"I told you that he started it," I replied. I pulled the knife from under my ribcage and inspected the wound. It looked as if it was already healing. I assumed that the colloidal silver would also ensure that I recovered quickly too.

"Is he going to live?" I asked. I wasn't really concerned about him. In fact, a lot of people's lives would be easier if he died. But I still didn't want his death on my conscience. It was selfish, but it was true.

"He's hurt, but not in danger," Sal answered. "Might need to visit one of the other Mistrys for medical attention."

I frowned. "This is bad, isn't it? How am I going to get out without being seen? I'm covered in blood, and he's barely breathing."

"I can try and teleport you back. My job here is done so I can leave," Sal said.

"What about Harper?"

"What about him?"

I shook my head. "He's outside."

Sal groaned. "What on earth is he doing here? Does he have a death wish?"

"Please."

"Right," Sal sighed. "You go out then, get him, and go. I… I'll sort the wolf-hunter out."

"What are you doing to do with him?" I frowned.

"Finish the job."

My eyes widened.

"Call an ambulance." He huffed. "My job was to protect him. Ironically. Now go, Mistry, before things get worse."

I nodded. "Thanks, Sal. I owe you."

"Lunch tomorrow," he called. "Common room. Midday."

I glanced back as my hand rested on the door handle. "Okay."

"And, Mistry," he added.

I looked up.

"Don't forget your photocopying. Use it to cover that bloodstain."

"Sal, I—"

"Taylor, go," he breathed. "Just grab your stuff and go. You've been through enough."

I wondered why he kept saying that. I wondered what he considered to be a normal amount of drama for a twenty-two, almost twenty-three year old. Maybe when the supernatural came into it, everything automatically became enough.

I grabbed my pile of photocopying and books and headed back out into the main library. I was cautious not to linger, so I dropped the books on the return trolley and just took the copies with me out to meet Harper. It took me a second to find him, or rather he found me.

"What happened?" he asked. It shouldn't have surprised me that he'd know that something had passed, but it did.

"I... can we just go? I'll tell you in the car."

He glanced down at my damp hair and the papers in my hands. I wondered if he was contemplating going in and finding out for himself.

"Harper, please," I whispered. "Trust me."

"Where are you parked?"

"Next street over, in the high-rise."

He looked back to the library then wrapped his arm around me. I heard the dull sizzling noise that my damp hair and top made against his skin, but he didn't remove it. Silver.

We walked fast, but not too fast, so I gathered that he could smell the blood and was wary of my condition. When we reached my car, I threw the papers and knife at my feet and sat down to inspect the wound. Other than bloodstains that was surprisingly human-looking, there was nothing. Not even a scar.

"*What* happened?" Harper exhaled. "Taylor—"

"I'm not… calm down, please," I said. "He… I… he's in worse shape than me."

Harper ran his hand recklessly through his hair. It stuck up in all directions.

"I knew that I should have gone with you. I knew that—"

"He had colloidal silver and a silver knife, Harper," I replied. "You wouldn't have walked out of there if you'd have stayed. At least silver doesn't hurt me."

"You're bleeding."

"Well, that's what happens when skin is broken. It's completely healed now, see?"

He frowned. "You're scarred."

I blushed. "That's not from the wound, that's from losing a lot of weight."

Stretch marks were something that I'd never been able to get rid of. They reminded me that I had achieved my goal, but had also put my body through something that it wasn't used to. For that, I both liked and despised them. They highlighted my weakness and my strength.

Harper moved his hand over my middle, and I rolled my bloodied shirt back down.

"Please, just drive," I sighed. "I don't want to be here when the ambulance shows up."

"Ambulance?"

"Sal was taking care of it."

"Sal was there?" He frowned. Then he understood. "Taylor, what—?"

My head shook. "He's not dead, Sal stopped me. I… please just start the car, Harper."

The car choked to life and I rested my head back. I wanted to tell him everything that had happened, but I couldn't form the words. I felt like I had failed as a human. I felt as if I should have had more control. I didn't want to hurt Theo, but I wanted him to leave me alone, leave us alone, and now I didn't know the consequences that I would face.

Harper didn't press me for details, so I wondered if the regret, or whatever it was, was painted on my face. He just held my hand and drove, weaving just above the speed limit through the heaviest traffic that South Coast had ever witnessed.

I didn't realise that we weren't headed to my unit until I saw the city buildings pass us.

"Are we going to Cole and Ruby's?" I asked. "Are the results back?"

"I live there too now, remember?" He smiled. "Plus, I can't take you home looking like that. Ruby might have something that you can wear."

I glanced down at my torn top. "Oh."

"Are you okay?"

"Yes, I told you that I'm already healed."

His head shook. "That's not what I asked. I asked if *you* were okay."

I exhaled. "I nearly killed him. I nearly killed a person."

"He attacked you."

"He threw colloidal silver on me," I answered. "I grabbed his throat. The knife... stabbing me was arguably self-defence."

"Why did he throw silver on *you*?" Harper asked. He always seemed to ask the question that I least expected him to. "He can't have thought that you were like me."

"No, he just knew that I was different. He wanted to know what I was."

"You didn't tell him, did you?"

I shook my head. "I didn't know if he knew about the hunter's dagger being the only thing that could kill me. He had that silver knife, and I didn't know if it was spelled, so I just played dumb. He knew that I was lying though, and I only confirmed his suspicions when he threw the silver liquid on me. I felt it strengthen me, and then it just made me mad."

"I'm sorry, I should have been there, or I shouldn't have come," he breathed. His hand squeezed mine. "It was my fault."

"Not everything is your fault, Harper. I get myself into these situations," I replied. "He is who he is, and that is not your fault. None of this is."

"But if it wasn't for me—"

"Stop, enough. Everything that has happened has led us to now. You and I are together now, and that... I'll never regret that."

Harper exhaled as he pulled into the underground car park of Cole's apartment block. There were the same few cars that were there, always blue cars, and then Cole's black Jag. Harper parked my silver four-wheel drive beside it and climbed out. I kicked the knife at my feet under the papers and followed suit.

Harper came straight around to me and wrapped his arms around me. Again, I heard the slight sizzle of his skin as it reacted with the silver fibres from the colloidal silver that had soaked me. I tried to push him away.

"Harper, it's hurting you," I mumbled.

"It's worth it."

I stopped fighting and hugged him back. "You still love me then?"

He huffed. "Why would I not?"

"Because I nearly strangled someone."

"I've done things that I'm not proud of too."

I pulled back. "But as a wolf. Harper, I was human. I was a human hurting another human. Who does that?"

"Stop judging yourself," he whispered. "I hate to sound like a philosopher, but sometimes there is no reason for things. Sometimes they just happen, and it's just because in the split of the moment, you willed it to happen. Not everything is thought out and pre-meditated. Making a bad decision in the heat of the moment doesn't make you a bad person. It makes you human."

"But I'm not really that human."

His hand cradled my cheek. "You look pretty human to me."

I rested my hand over his heart. "So do you."

"Taylor? What happened?" Ruby called from across the garage. "Are you hurt?"

I looked up. Vampires.

"No. I was, but I'm healed," I answered. "You wouldn't happen to have a spare shirt that I can wear?"

"I have too many, thanks to Lesleigh." Ruby laughed. Lesleigh was a vampire-fashion designer that was an old friend of Cole's. I hadn't heard too much about her, but Ruby missed her when she was abroad.

"Come inside," she said.

Harper took my hand and led me towards where she was standing by the lift. Ruby frowned as I got closer.

"Do I want to ask?"

I shook my head. "I did a bad thing."

"Haven't we all?" She smiled. We stepped into the lift, and her hand reached to touch the ends of my hair, but I twisted away.

"Colloidal silver," I said. "Nothing personal."

Her brow pinched. "That sounds a little personal. Who did this to you?"

"The Greek," Harper growled. "He's lucky that he already needed an ambulance."

"Oh, dear."

I rubbed my face. "I'm just thankful that Sal was there to stop me."

"Sal? Why?" Ruby asked. "Oh. Oh, dear, Taylor."

Harper hugged me against him, and I buried myself into his chest.

"I'm sure he'll be okay," Ruby said quietly. "And by the looks of you, it was self-defence."

I didn't bother correcting her, because a large part of me wanted her to believe that I wasn't as terrible as I actually was.

"By the way, Harper, Cole has your bloodwork back," Ruby said. "We were about to call you both."

I looked up. "And?"

"And Cole will explain it properly. I'm rubbish at medical things, despite my experience around hospitals."

I nodded and looked up as the light glowed from the top level. Ruby had told me once that, as a human, she had been diagnosed with lupus at a young age, and was in and out of hospitals. As fate would have it, Cole had been the one to treat her as a child and then, after years, they reunited as adults. There were a lot of obstacles that they had to overcome before they became the Ruby and Cole that Harper and I knew today, but I couldn't imagine them as anything else.

"What happened?" Cole asked as the doors opened. "Taylor, you're bleeding."

"Was," I sighed. "I healed."

He nodded. "Come. Let me check your vitals."

"I'm fine, really," I answered. "Ruby said that you have Harper's results back."

Cole frowned at me. "Yes, and I'll go through them in detail as long as you tell me why you are covered in blood and silver."

I exhaled. "Deal. So what did they indicate? Is he immortal or is... can... will... is he the same as he was before?"

"The results indicate that the change we saw in Harper's blood after being wounded is no longer present," he explained. "I would deduce that it may have been a reaction to the stab wound that he was recovering from. Those healing entities had spiked and were still active in his blood when it was tested. He hasn't changed genetically, and I daresay that he will not."

I blinked and folded my arms. Cole looked almost apologetic as he waited for me to reply. Harper, too, was more concerned about my reaction than what he'd just heard. He seemed a little unaffected by the news.

"So..." I frowned. "Are you telling me that I stabbed Harper for nothing? Why did his light disappear then? Does that mean that I can still reap him in the Full Moon?"

"Taylor, I—" Cole started.

"Here," Ruby said. She held out a glass of milk and a bag of mixed nuts and seeds towards me. "It's skim milk and vitamin B. You lost some blood earlier. I always found it helped with the energy levels."

I didn't feel like eating or drinking at all, but Ruby was so thoughtful that I took it anyway. I sat down on one of the Chesterfields.

"I understand that you have many questions, Taylor," Cole said thoughtfully. "But I'm afraid that I'm not one who can answer them all. I apologise that I got your hopes up previously, but all indications would suggest that Harper is still very much a mortal werewolf that could be a target for a banshee."

I shook my head. "But—"

"But that is the only thing that's changed, Taylor," Harper interrupted. "Yes, I can be killed, I could always be killed, and yes, I will age, but I expected to since birth. As for being a target from you, as I said when we first found out your fate, I am not afraid. I trust in our future, yours and mine together."

I frowned at the milk between my fingers. "I just thought that maybe you would be protected if you were ageless."

"Weavers and Lacers are ageless, but they are not really protected from you, Taylor," Harper said. "In fact, I am rather glad that I'll age as normal. Watching you grow old and not being able to experience that with you would have been very difficult."

I'd never thought about that. I should have, but I didn't.

"That's true." I nodded. "We can experience being senile together."

"More so." He smiled. "Since all of this is confusing enough."

Harper knelt down in front of me. He took the glass from my hands and put it on the coffee table behind him.

"Such is fate, yes?" he whispered. "Such is life."

I leant over to rest my forehead on his. "Okay."

"Not to be a dampener," Ruby said.

I looked up at her and Harper rocked back on his heels. He picked up the glass of milk and took a sip as he sat beside me on the couch.

"Sorry," Ruby replied. "But are we certain that you *can* age, Taylor? I mean, I don't know how old Alba was, or how she appeared as a human, but if Sal is right and she could only die when she was killed, then what's to say that she doesn't age?"

I hadn't thought of that either.

Harper looked equally as perplexed as I felt, but as Ruby glanced at Cole, I noticed that he didn't seem that surprised by her question.

"But... but Sal ages like normal." I blinked. "He..."

Sure, he aged like normal, but he once told me that he became a reaper by the reaper before showing mercy on him and handing over the torch. Sal could arguably pass on the job, and pass on whenever he chose to. Me, a banshee, they had to be killed to pass the buck, as far as I knew. Regular life may not come with a manual, but at least you could learn things from other people's experience. That didn't exactly work the same way when you were a supernatural creature that was unique in its own right. I had a job, I had my own characteristics. I just didn't know where to start looking for what they were.

"Oh," I sighed. "Oh no. You're right. I have no idea if I can age. There are so many things that I haven't thought of. I don't know hardly anything about being a banshee."

Ruby pressed her lips together. "Cole, sweet, do you think that Miguel or anyone would know anything about banshees? Surely someone knows something. Taylor isn't the only one out there, after all."

Cole nodded. "I have mentioned Taylor to him before, but I will ask him again. Europe has a higher population of the supernatural so he will be in a better position to search."

75

I looked down at the bag of seeds and nuts on my knees and grabbed a handful. They weren't my first choice of snack— usually I'd go for carrot sticks or something low in calories— but now was clearly not the time to worry about food. Besides, if I weren't going to age, I would literally have forever to manage my weight.

"Taylor, it's going to be okay," Harper murmured. He took the bag from my hands and tossed it on the table. I liked that he knew that I'd regret the handful later, but for now, I felt like I needed to comfort-eat.

"I don't know. I don't know if it will be. I just—" My words were cut off as my phone chimed. I patted my pockets and pulled it out. It was a text from Sal.

"The hunter will live. His windpipe is a bit busted though, can't talk. You're out of the woods. SV."

I exhaled and slid my phone onto the table. Harper rocked forward to read the screen.

"That's something," he sighed. "The wolf-hunter is alive but can't speak."

I shook my head and stood. I couldn't believe that someone being incapacitated was actually good news for me. How did I get like this? What the heck was I worried about carbohydrates and stretchmarks for? This was a whole other realm of problems.

"What exactly happened with the Greek hunter?" Cole asked.

I glanced back at Harper, then at Ruby. My gaze dropped to the hole in my top.

"I lost control."

Cole nodded in understanding, as a small smile caused his cheeks to dimple. "Haven't we all?"

Phase Three

The Collector

I stayed with Harper in his apartment that was on the eleventh floor of Cole's building. Apparently, it was just outside of comfortable earshot for vampires and werewolves, as long as they didn't concentrate on hearing further.

"Harper," I murmured into his collarbone. I was wrapped in his hold, and the heat was enough to keep me warm without a blanket. Regardless, I liked sleeping with blankets, so we had the air conditioner on to balance out the temperature.

"Taylor," he replied. His hands ran down my arm, and I shivered.

"Why didn't you hear Theo and me before?" I asked. "I mean, I'm glad that you didn't because then you would be wrapped up in this too, but we weren't far away from where you were. I thought that you might have been listening out for me."

He frowned. "I was. I heard you go into the copy room."

"How did you know that it was me?"

"You have distinctive footfalls."

"Oh," I sighed. "So you *were* listening? Did you hear Theo come in?"

He shook his head. "No. One of my tutors from last semester spotted me and came over to talk. It was only when you were coming out that my attention wasn't divided and I could concentrate on hearing more. It's very difficult to listen out when distracted. Letting in too many noises can be overwhelming."

I nodded. "What happens if he tells someone that it was me?"

"He can't speak."

"That means nothing, he could write it out."

Harper was silent for a moment. "He won't tell."

"He could though," I mumbled. "He might have stabbed me, but I'm completely healed. Out of the two of us, he's worse off. He could claim that I just grabbed him and—"

"And held his neck so tight that you collapsed his windpipe?" he offered. "You?"

I shuffled. "You don't think that people will believe I could?"

"No, I don't think that anyone would believe that you *would*. What reason would you have to attack him? Taylor Mistry, the daughter of an acclaimed South Coast surgeon, a defender of animals, and an upstanding veterinary science student?"

I frowned. "I'm hardly an upstanding student. I'm only doing winter term because I need to make up credit points."

"You are missing my point, Taylor." He smiled. "Besides, even though hunters work with the express purpose to put an end to the supernatural, they also make it a point not to broadcast our existence."

"That's weird to me. Like, you would think that sharing your secret would cause a large-scale witch-hunt, but instead they keep it to themselves and struggle on alone."

His eyebrows lifted. "Well, for that I am thankful. But honestly, if you hadn't seen what you have seen, and if you were not what you are, would you believe it if they told you?"

My lips pressed together. "I see your point."

I rested my head back on his chest and listened as his heart flipped against his ribcage. He was so vital and alive, so warm and central to my universe that I couldn't fathom ever living in a world where he wasn't here. He was like my sun, without him, everything would be in shadows, cold and barren. I never wanted to move from that spot because I felt as though his heartbeats were numbered, and I didn't want to miss even one of them.

"Taylor, what's wrong?" he asked. His deep voice rumbled under my ear, and I looked up at him.

"What do you mean?"

His fingers tucked my hair behind my ear. "Your heart rate suddenly got faster, and that only means two things. Considering your lips are turned down and not silencing mine, then I can only deduce that you are worrying about something."

I felt the frown on my face and tried to tip it upside. "I love you. I was just thinking that I love you."

Darkness fell over his olive-green eyes. "That saddens you?"

"No, the thought of living without you saddens me."

"That won't happen."

I shook my head. "Don't say that when you don't know for sure that it's true."

He shuffled to half sit up. "Don't say that I am already gone when I'm not. I'm right here, Taylor. I'm here with you now. Now is all that matters to me, and I'm going to try as hard as I can to make now last for as long as possible."

"I didn't mean to wish our time together away," I sighed. "I just meant that I don't know what is going to happen on the next Full Moon, or tomorrow, or a few hours from now, but I want this, us, to last. I want to grow old with you, and I don't want to feel like you and I are living from Full Moon to Full Moon."

He shook his head. "That's the way it will always be for me. Ever since I was bitten, this is what I am. I live by the Moon, and I will probably die by the Moon. But, as long as I get to spend every other moment that I have with you, then that is enough for me. You and I, here and now. That is enough."

I rested my hand on his chest and noticed that his heart was beating faster than before.

"I'm sorry," I whispered. I felt his heart stutter then thump a little harder.

"Why?"

"I keep ruining our moments together by bringing this up. I'm just terrified of losing you," I murmured. I felt his heart slow a little.

"*Oui*, I know," he answered. "I have the same concerns, only I try not to think too much about them. I can't control what happens, but I can control the way that I respond to the knowledge. I choose to be happy now and I worry when I have the cause to. *C'est la vie.*"

"That's life," I breathed. "Live in the moment."

"To the fullest extent."

I smiled and felt his heartbeat quicken again. I wondered if he could hear mine respond to it.

His smile turned into a small chuckle. "No more worries?"

My head shook. "Not right now."

His eyes fell to my hand on his chest. "Your heart is still racing."

"Well, that can only mean one thing then."

He looked up, and I leant over to catch my lips on his. Our hearts leapt in unison, and nothing more was said.

*

"Taylor Maye Mistry," Sal said as I stumbled through into the common room. It was after midday on Tuesday, but my morning tutorial had run a little late. The half-hour it took me to get here was probably my fault, but I wasn't looking forward to seeing him after what had happened. I didn't want to see the judgement in his face, or worse, his understanding. I didn't know why Sal's opinion of me mattered so much, but I suppose everyone just wanted to be accepted by everyone else, regardless of who they were.

"Hey, Sal. Salvatore Vincent."

"What kept you? Everything okay, I hope." He smiled. I always found it remarkable that he could smile after everything that he has witnessed, seen, or been a part of. I supposed if he didn't, then he'd be admitted into a mental health facility. I admired that quality in Sal – seeing the light in the darkness.

"Sorry, I got held up in class," I sighed. "Nothing serious."

"Glad to hear it. For a change."

I dropped my bag at my feet and flopped on the bench seat. "Well, get it over with then."

Sal frowned. "Get what over with?"

"The lecture, or whatever you wanted to see me for."

"Lecture? I'm not a teacher here, Mistry. You'll have to pay someone else for a lesson if that's what you're after."

I blinked. "So what was lunch about?"

"I told you, I miss hanging out. No one else really knows about what I am any more, and it sort of nice when you don't have to keep up the pretence with someone."

I nodded slowly, thinking of how Hunter had told me that was what Harper had been for her. Ruby had mentioned once that Lesleigh and Cole were somewhat of a team before she became a vampire, and then there was me. Sure, I had Harper now, but it was different. He didn't face and experience death the way that I had to. Sal did.

"I know what you mean." I nodded.

"Sure you do." He huffed. "Your boyfriend is a werewolf, your bestie is a vampire, and you have slumber parties with a Weaver. You must be really lonely as a banshee."

I shook my head. "It's not the same, and you know it. Why else would you have shown up at the cemetery last Full Moon?"

He smiled. "Are you saying that we're friends, Taylor Maye Mistry?"

"Salvatore Vincent, you are—"

"I know, I know. I am cute, and amazing, wise, and attractive."

I tipped my head. "I seriously think that you misinterpret everything I say."

He chuckled. "I'm just reading between the lines."

"Sometimes there's nothing between the lines, Sal. Sometimes what's there is just what's there."

"Ever the scientist." He smirked. "Can I get you something for lunch? Beef burger? Salad? Wolf-hunter?"

I frowned. "Too soon."

"Too sensitive."

"I brought my own… crap," I groaned. No, I didn't. I usually would have packed my own lunch, but I'd stayed with Harper, and he hadn't gotten around to stocking his newly bought fridge.

"Crap? I don't think they sell that here," Sal replied. "But there's a place down the road that might."

"You are so ridiculous," I sighed.

He laughed. "What do you eat? I noticed that you're a bit picky."

"I can get something later; you don't have to buy me anything."

"Don't be stupid, it's lunchtime now. Just tell me what you like."

"A salad sandwich of some description, or even a wrap," I shrugged. "Seriously, Sal, I can buy my own lunch."

He rolled his eyes. "You can get the next one. What meat stuff do you like? Chicken, or ham, or what?"

"Either."

"Not too picky then, Mistry."

"But preferably no butter or mayonnaise, and not toasted."

He smirked. "I take that back."

I exhaled. "I told you that I can get it myself."

"Anything to drink?"

"I have water."

He shook his head. "Of course you do. I'll be right back."

I rolled my eyes and pulled my phone out. I really wanted to send Jesse a text, but I didn't know what to say. I'd told him that I wouldn't be home last night and he hadn't replied. I thought that maybe he might have been at work, but he'd never *not* responded to me before. I very fleetingly considered texting Brandon, since he always seemed to be at my place, but then thought better of it. After our last conversation, he probably wouldn't reply to me anyway.

"Wolfie keeping tabs on you?" Sal asked. He sat down opposite and nudged a low-fat ham, cheese, and salad wrap towards me.

"No, more me keeping tabs on my brother," I answered. "Nice selection. I approve."

"Lord have mercy, she approves," he sang. "So, why do you need to keep tabs on your brother?"

I frowned at my phone and then reached for the wrap. "He's still hurting after Ashley's death. He's not telling me anything."

"People grieve differently."

"That's what Harper said."

Sal nodded. "But you're still worried?"

"He's never shut me out before. He's even shutting his best friend out—"

"That blond guy, right?"

I groaned. "Right, Brandon."

Sal smiled a little. "So, he's not speaking to anyone?"

"That's the thing, I think he is, but I don't know who," I sighed. "Every time I ask him about it, he just bites my head off. I don't need to know his every movement or who it's with, but I'm a little curious as to why he won't tell me. We normally tell each other everything."

"*Everything?*"

I rolled my eyes. "Well, almost everything."

"That's a little hypocritical, isn't it?"

"No, I keep things from him because he's better off not knowing." I shrugged. "He's keeping things from me because he thinks that I'll judge him for whatever he's doing with whoever he's seeing."

Sal laughed.

I frowned. "What's funny?"

"Nothing," he sighed. "Look, if you're that worried about him, why don't you just follow him?"

"Stalk him?"

"Tail him."

"I'm not tracking my brother's movements," I murmured. "He'll tell me when he's ready."

Sal nodded. "So don't worry about it."

"He's my twin, I'll always worry."

"Taylor, he's an adult, he was raised well, and he's trying to deal with one of the hardest things that a human will ever

86

experience," he said. "I don't know him personally, but I think I know you pretty well. If he's anything like you, then I don't think that you have anything too bad to worry about."

I smiled weakly. "Thanks."

He nodded and looked down at the white paper bag in front of him. I opened my wrap and took a bite, while Sal pulled out something huge wrapped in more white paper.

"What is that?"

"Chicken burger."

"Did they fit an entire chicken in there?"

He unwrapped it and appraised it. "Hm, looks like only half a chicken."

"Is that all you're having? No entrée? No soup? No eight more courses?"

"Well, I've already had a muffin, a fruit salad, and some wedges before," he replied. He took a giant bite and then attempted to chew it. It looked painful. "I was thinking of getting a waffle afterwards if you're keen. Otherwise, there's that new frozen yoghurt place opened around the corner which I've been meaning to try."

"Where do you put all that food?"

"You're a scientist, Mistry, where do you think?"

I shook my head. "You defy science, Sal."

He took another bite and then offered it to me.

I frowned at it. "No, I'm good. The wrap is more than enough for me."

"More than enough."

"What?"

"Don't you want more sometimes?" he asked. "I mean, even sometimes, don't you feel like trying something different?"

I wondered if we were still talking about food and then decided that I didn't want to consider that he could be talking about something else.

"No," I said. "I like what I have."

His orange eyes appraised me for a moment, and I saw something in them that probably shouldn't be there. But maybe I was wrong. I hoped that I was wrong. Although he was irritating sometimes, I really did enjoy his company. If he was harbouring anything more than friendship for me, then I knew that it would make everything more complicated. I couldn't handle more complication in my life.

"Sal, can I ask you something?"

His eyebrows lifted. "Do you think that I'd say no?"

"Do you know if banshees age?"

"If they *age*?"

I nodded. "I mean, will I be stuck this way until someone kills me, or can I grow old and die?"

His head shook. "I don't know. I… Alba didn't say much. We only caught up to exchange stories a couple of times, so I really don't know anything more than I've already told you."

"Okay."

"Sorry."

I took a bite of my wrap and chewed it twice before swallowing. It caught in my throat, and I cringed as I tried to get it down.

Sal bit his lip.

"Have you ever thought about how strange it is that banshees reap werewolves?" he asked. "I mean, they age as normal and are hunted by the wolf-hunters. Most of them now are too well-behaved to bite people, so I don't really see the point in them *also* being picked off by banshees. It just seems a little unfair."

I raised an eyebrow. "Are you Team Wolf now?"

"I'm Team... what?" Sal blinked. "I'm Team Reaper, of course. But, like, think about it. What's the point of targeting such an endangered species? It would be like reaping Light Lacers."

I shrugged. "I don't understand a lot of it, to be honest."

"True. It's all a little too philosophical for you."

I threw his balled-up paper bag at his head, and it bounced off.

"Hey!" he squeaked. "Watch it, Mistry."

I laughed. "Hey, Sal?"

"*Sì?*"

I rolled my eyes. "Thanks."

"For what?"

"For lunch, for being a friend, for stopping me from killing Theo yesterday."

He smiled weakly. "Don't mention it, Mistry."

"I mean it though, I don't know what I would have done if—"

"Don't mention it," he sighed. "Don't think about it; don't consider the alternatives; don't dwell on it. You can't control any of it now. What's done is done."

I nodded. "You're right."

"That happens on occasion."

"Rare occasion." I smiled.

He shoved the remaining edge of his burger in his mouth and, again, tried to chew it.

"What did you do with him? Did you call an ambulance?" I asked.

Sal finished chewing and swallowed. "Eventually."

"Eventually?"

He shrugged. "Sure. I took some of the pain away, then cleaned up the place and left. When I was back in the dorms, I called for an ambulance."

My eyebrows lifted. "How long did you wait?"

"It was only like two minutes," he sighed. "I'm a fast worker."

"I should be mad, but he's still alive, so I guess no harm was done," I murmured. "Plus I did worse so…"

He huffed. "Yeah, true. Don't throw stones at my glasshouse, Mistry."

I smiled. "Can I ask you another favour?"

"More?"

"It's what friends do, right?"

His eyes rolled. "Sure."

"I um, I need to go into the library to get those books that I was looking at yesterday, and maybe photocopy pages from the ones I can't loan," I sighed. "The thing is though, well, I don't really want to go there alone."

"Why? Theo's in hospital."

I shook my head. "I'm just scared of going back to where it all happened."

"Oh." He nodded. "Sure, I'll go with you."

"Thanks. I'll buy you frozen yoghurt afterwards."

"Score." He chuckled. His smile faded. "Uh-oh."

I groaned. "Don't tell me that duty calls."

"I wish."

"What?" I frowned. I followed his eye line and smiled at Harper. "Hey, what are you doing here?"

Harper tipped his head. "Lunch, but I see that you have beaten me to it. Hello, Grim."

"Wolf."

I rolled my eyes.

"Are you finished here?" Harper asked. "I've finally completed furnishing my apartment. I even have food in the fridge."

I pressed my lips together. "I actually need to go to the library. I didn't get done what I needed to yesterday."

"Okay, we'll go there first."

I glanced at Sal whose eyebrows were lifted.

"Oh, sorry, as long as you are finished," Harper added.

"No, please. You two go and do what you've got to do," Sal sighed. "I'm going to go knit, or something."

"But I was going to get you frozen yoghurt." I frowned. "Don't you want it any more?"

Sal stood. "Raincheck."

"Thanks again for lunch."

"Always a pleasure, Taylor Mistry."

I watched him go and waved as he gave a departing glance over his shoulder. Harper came with me to the library to get what I needed to, and then we both went back to the apartment building. We were just getting in the lift when I got that feeling again.

The breathlessness.

Harper rested his hands on my shoulders as my hands clawed at my chest. It was the worst that I'd ever felt, not only the air was being sucked away, but like it was being replaced with some kind of liquid. I caved into his arms and screamed into his shoulder. My hands clutched for him, and I didn't realise that my nails were sinking into his skin until I heard him yelp. We both fell at the same time, though, while I dropped to the floor, Harper clutched at the handrail, mashing the number for Cole's apartment before reaching to scan his hand on the plate.

"I'm sorry, I'm so sorry," I mouthed. I had no air, and my bloodstained fingers shook.

"No, it's not your fault," Harper panted.

The doors opened, and Ruby stood in the doorway.

"Oh my gosh," she gasped. "Taylor, Harper… Taylor, was that you?"

"Help Harper, I think I hurt him," I wheezed. "Is Cole here?"

Ruby dashed to take Harper's weight and assisted him into the lounge room. She sat him at the table.

"Cole is at the office, I'll call him," she answered.

Harper nodded. "Check Taylor, see that she's okay."

"I'm fine, I… I'm so sorry, Harper."

Ruby hung up her phone and turned to me. "Taylor, go and clean yourself up. I'll find you a change of clothes."

I didn't understand what she meant until I glanced down and saw my jeans and top were splatted with blood. Again.

"We need to clean his wounds," I said. "They'll heal faster if they're clean. The silver in my nails affects him. I need to clean the wounds first."

Ruby nodded, a frown etched into her marble-like skin. "Okay, I'll find Cole's medical kit."

"Thank you."

I hastened over to Harper and tried to lift up his T-shirt to see the damage. He winced, so I dropped it again. Cutting it off would be less painful for him. I spun to search for scissors as Ruby appeared back at my side with Cole's black bag. I smiled tightly at her, and then fossicked through, finding what I needed, and began cutting away the material. The puncture wounds that my nails had made were crescents around his shoulders. It astounded me the damage that I'd done in a few seconds.

"Oh crap, it's really deep," I sighed. "I'm so sorry, Harper."

He blinked up at me with puppy-dog eyes. "Stop apologising. I'll heal."

I bit my lip and looked through the bag, finding some gauze and disinfectant.

"This might sting a little." I frowned.

"No more than silver nails," he breathed. He tried to smile, but I couldn't find any humour in anything that was happening.

My head shook, and I blinked back tears as he sucked air through his teeth.

"I keep my nails short, they shouldn't do this," I muttered.

"What happened, Taylor?" Ruby asked. "Did you have another, um, attack?"

I wiped my damp eye with my wrist. "It was worse than the other times. I couldn't stop it. I couldn't breathe. I felt like my lungs were filling with water."

Ruby looked down. "I've felt that before."

"Really? When?"

"When I was dying," she answered. "When I was human."

I frowned and went back to dabbing the punctures. When I was convinced that they were silver-free, I dropped the gauze in the plastic bag that Ruby had found for me, and wiped my hands on my jeans. They were already stained anyway.

Harper sat back and looked up at me. "Stop, Taylor."

"Stop what?"

"Stop blaming yourself," he replied. "I will be okay."

My head shook. "I hurt you."

"It was my fault. I grabbed you first. I thought that maybe I could help."

"Now you stop, Harper. Don't you go blaming yourself for another one of my oversights."

Ruby exhaled. "Cole is back."

I heard the lift door open and light footsteps as the blond vampire appeared in the doorway.

"What happened?"

"I screamed, I hurt Harper," I said. "I cleaned his wounds so they'll heal quicker. I figured that the silver from my nails might be around the puncture sites."

Cole nodded. "Good idea. Are you all right, Taylor?"

"I'm not hurt."

"That's not what I asked."

I shook my head. "This is getting out of control. I don't know how to make it stop. I don't know when it's coming, I just start gasping for air, and then it overcomes me."

Cole's reassuring hand rested on my shoulder. "You should go and get yourself cleaned up. I'll inspect Harper's wounds in the meantime, all right?"

I nodded. "Sorry for calling you away from work."

He smiled. "It's no bother, really."

"Come, Taylor. I'll find you something to wear," Ruby said. Her hand reached towards me, and I took it to steady my shaky legs. The coolness of her skin was refreshing, like coming up for air.

The only thing of Ruby's that fit me was a dress that was a little shapeless but still considered *high-end-fashion*. It was another blow to me today, finding out that I no longer fit into her clothes. Even if she was a little shorter than me, I used to be able to still wear her shirts and shorts. It just confirmed my suspicions that I had put on weight in the last couple of weeks. It shouldn't have upset me as much as it did, but I found myself unable to stop the stupid tears.

"It's okay, Taylor," Ruby soothed.

My head shook. "I'm fat, and I'm toxic, and I can't stop screaming. I kill innocent supernatural people once a month… and I nearly killed a *human being* yesterday."

"Oh, honey," he sighed. Her cold arms moved around me. "You can't be so hard on yourself. Over half of those things you don't have any control over."

"But I worked so hard, I gave it everything, I pushed myself to the limits, and now it's all for nothing. I do have control over what I eat, but I still messed it up."

She looked up at me and then rested her hands on my shoulders. "You listen to me, you did not mess anything up. You did what you had to when you had to. You said so yourself, Taylor, some things you can't control. The things that you can control, you're allowed to get wrong. Just learn from it. Get it right next time. It's not the end."

"But it was so hard before, I don't know if I can do it again."

"Taylor, you have faced banshees, wendigoes, and wolf-hunters, you can do anything." She smiled. "Now come on, let's see how Harper is."

I swallowed and nodded. She took my hand and tugged me out.

"Tah-dah," Ruby said. I felt even more self-conscious than before. Mostly because I didn't feel comfortable in the dress – even if they told me that I looked good in it. I knew that it was a lie.

"Lovely." Cole nodded.

"As always," Harper added.

I looked down at the pale blue dress. "It's a sack."

Ruby laughed. "That looks like sack even on me."

"Wash your mouth out with silver," a ringing voice chimed. I looked up and saw a vision of perfection standing in the doorway. She was clearly a vampire, all pale skin, and bright silver eyes, light brown hair that fell to her tiny waist, and she literally just looked like she had just stepped off a runway.

"Lesleigh," Ruby gushed. She darted over and pounced on the girl who was even shorter than she was. I'd heard a lot about Lesleigh White, the infamous fashion-designer who was a mentor to Ruby, and family to Cole. She had been in Spain for the entire time that I'd known the South Coast vampires.

"Leigh, you're back." Cole smiled. "Did you come alone?"

"Well, hello to you too, Nicolas." Lesleigh grinned. "I'm great, thanks for asking."

Cole exhaled. "*Hola*, Lesleigh. *Cómo estás?*"

"*Muy bien, Nico. Cómo es todo aquí?*"

"Everything has been rather interesting here," Cole answered. "As you well know."

"Is Miguel here too?" Ruby asked. She was still clutching Lesleigh as if letting go of her would result in her materialising into the shadows.

"No, I came back with Hunter."

"Hunter?" Harper frowned. He leant forward, and I could see that the holes that my fingers had made were almost fully healed. They had taken longer than usual, but that was because silver had caused it. They would also scar like the other scratches I had caused, though that was under a very different circumstance.

Lesleigh glanced at him. "Yes. She came to Spain after what happened with the banshee."

I shuffled, and Lesleigh glanced at me. "Which I'm guessing is the doe-eyed brunette who doesn't like my designs."

"Leigh, this is Taylor Mistry," Ruby said. "She is a good friend of mine, as well as a banshee."

Lesleigh smiled. "Hello, Taylor. Cole has told me a lot about you. He is a collector of people like you."

I glanced at Cole. "Collector?"

"He knows a lot of supernatural people," Lesleigh explained. "More so than Miguel, and he has been around for centuries."

"I do not collect people in a creepy way. I just enjoy learning about what is out there, and the customs of the various species," Cole replied. "Pay no attention to Lesleigh, Taylor, she has no filter."

Lesleigh made a face.

Ruby smiled between the two of them. It looked like she had witnessed a lot of the sibling-type bantering between the two them over the last few years. I couldn't help but relate it back to the way that Jesse and I were now. It was a far cry from the way that we had been before Ashley's death.

"So what made you come back now, Leigh?" Ruby asked. "Is it because of Hunter, or do you have some news about banshees?"

Lesleigh looked around the room and stared at Harper. "Why do you look familiar?"

"Oh, Leigh, this is Harper Lovett," Ruby replied. "He's—"

"Lovett?" Lesleigh repeated. "As in *Lincoln* Lovett?"

Harper frowned. "He was my great-grandfather."

Lesleigh smirked. "I see."

"How do you know my great-grandfather?"

I blinked. "Wait, there's an oval in South Iris named Lincoln Lovett Oval, isn't there?"

I hadn't thought about it before. It was silly, but considering South Coast was so small, you would think that I'd have noticed that my boyfriend's surname was on one of the local landmarks.

"I think you mean that *Cole* named an oval in South Iris after him," Lesleigh answered.

Harper's frown deepened. "Why? Who is he to you, Cole?"

All eyes traced to Cole.

"Lincoln was my cousin. We grew up together in the south of England."

Harper blinked. "Did you know anyone else in my family?"

"You mean *his* family?" Lesleigh said. She wasn't being helpful.

The look that Cole gave her told me that he seemed to agree with me.

"I didn't know your father or grandfather personally, but I did try to keep tabs on them over the years. I didn't see Lincoln after I was turned, and I always regretted leaving him. Unfortunately, going back was not in his best interest. I didn't meet your great-grandmother either, Lina-Marie was her name, but I do know that she was also a wolf."

Harper's mouth fell open. "What?"

"How do you know that?" I asked.

"I knew her sister," Cole said.

Ruby looked up. "Diana?"

He nodded, and I got the feeling that I was missing something.

"If she… if my great-grandmother was a wolf, then does that mean that Lincoln or—"

"Lina-Marie never turned him, but I believe that most of their children turned," Cole explained. "They had five, only one male though – your grandfather, their youngest. He went on to have—"

"Five children, my father was the youngest," Harper nodded. "He was turned by his Aunty."

"And you?" Lesleigh asked.

"I am an only child, my father bit me when I was four," he replied.

"And your mother?"

"Human."

"Really?" Lesleigh mused. "I thought that the wolf-gene was only passed on to females, Cole?"

"What do you mean?" Harper frowned. "There is no wolf-gene."

"Then how are they still around? From biting?" Lesleigh huffed. "Wolves are too restrained to bite people nowadays, and they need to preserve their species somehow. Perhaps you only *assumed* that there is no gene since it was not passed on to you. Your mother wasn't a wolf and you, sir, are male."

Harper looked to Cole for an explanation. It seemed as though he was a bit frustrated by Lesleigh's curt explanation.

"She's right, Lycanthropy is passed through the female bloodline," Cole said. "My apologies, friend. I didn't think that it was something that you were unaware of. It is no secret that there are more female werewolves than males."

Harper blinked. "Are you sure?"

"Yes, Harper, quite sure. As I said, I knew the sister of your great-grandmother. We were quite close."

"So every female on my father's side was a wolf?"

"He didn't tell you?" I asked. "Your father, I mean, he never mentioned anything about your family history?"

Harper shook his head. "He didn't talk much about them. I do not even know if he knew."

"Of course he would know if he was turned by his Aunty." Lesleigh huffed.

"Leigh, you're not being helpful," Cole said.

"That seems to be going around," she sighed. "So I guess you didn't think to tell little Lovett that you're distant cousins then?"

Cole glanced at Harper. "I didn't want to overwhelm you. It is strange enough that I am a vampire old enough to grow up with your great-grandfather without telling you we are of the same bloodline."

"It might have overwhelmed me, but I would have liked to have known. I don't know a lot about my ancestry. My mother died young and, as I said, my father never spoke about them."

"My apologies," Cole whispered. "I should have said."

"I just didn't think that I had any family left," Harper breathed. "Rob may be family to me, but he is not blood-related."

Harper's head lowered and I saw the glow around him began to lighten. Despite my hesitation to be close to Harper after hurting him before, I hated seeing him with that look of desolation on his face. I didn't know if the glow meant that I shouldn't be near him, but it didn't matter now. He needed me.

I crossed the room and tipped his chin up. He sat back and then wrapped his arms around my middle as if holding me would save his life. I moved my arms around his scruffy hair and hugged him back as best I could.

"It's okay, I'm here," I murmured. "You're not alone, Harper."

I felt the warmth in his arms as I smoothed my hands down his back. The wounds in his shoulders were healed entirely now – his light was also dimming again too.

"They're an unlikely pair, aren't they?" Lesleigh said. "Cute, but well unlikely."

"They are the perfect fit," Ruby replied. "Like another couple that I know."

I looked up as Cole slipped in beside his blonde counterpart and pressed his lips to her temple.

Lesleigh made another face. "Ugh, couples are lame when I'm not in them."

Phase Four

The Raven of Knowledge

Harper and I didn't hang around at Cole's apartment for much longer after Lesleigh arrived. It was evident that they all had a lot of catching up to do, and I needed to get home to study. I drove Harper back to his Honda Shadow motorbike, which was still parked at the university. When I pulled up and I turned off my car engine, Harper didn't make any attempt to move.

"I'll follow you home," he murmured. "I want to make sure that you get there okay."

"I'm fine, really. I feel fine."

He nodded. "You feel fine until you don't."

I looked down. "How are you feeling?"

"I am completely healed."

"Good. I am so sorry—"

"Please," he sighed. His fingers reached to tip my chin towards him. "Stop apologising. I know that you meant me no harm. It's a lucky thing that I can heal fast."

"Kind of," I mumbled.

"Taylor."

I grabbed his hand. "Harper, how would you feel if the situation was reversed, and it was you who hurt me? Tell me, how would you feel?"

His head shook.

"Anyway, I need to catch up with my assignments," I whispered. "Um, what's tomorrow? Wednesday. I'm helping out at the vet clinic tomorrow, but maybe we could do dinner and a movie? Unless you've got other plans."

He breathed a laugh. "What other plans would I have?"

"I thought that maybe you would want to see Hunter now that she's back."

"Hunter stabbed me the last time that I saw her."

"Well, I put ten holes in you a couple of hours ago." I shrugged. "I'm sure she feels bad about it. She's your person."

His eyebrows lifted. "My person?"

"Yeah, she's your Lesleigh. She's the one who's been there for you over the years, the one who understood when you had no one else. She told me once that she stopped counting the years when she met you."

"She tried to attack you too, Taylor."

"You mean when I tried to kill her?" I huffed. "I'm not perfect, Harper, I'm nowhere close."

He smiled. "You are perfect to me."

I shook my head. I felt the same way about him, but I hated hearing it aimed at me. What happened when he realised that I wasn't perfect?

"I'll follow you home and see you tomorrow," Harper said. He leant over and cupped my face, but I recoiled.

"What's wrong?"

"Sorry," I sighed. I rested my hand on his and leant forward to kiss him. His hand moved down to my sternum, and I could feel my heart thumping against it.

"I'm just terrified that I'm going to hurt you again," I breathed. "I love you. I don't ever want to hurt you."

"I trust you," he whispered. "And as long as you don't kill me, we'll get through it."

My eyes closed. "That's not funny."

He kissed me quickly again. "I love you. Good luck tomorrow. Drive safe."

"You too."

Harper leant back and opened the door, slipping into the evening air towards his bike. I waited until he had started it up before starting my car again.

The sun was just setting when I got home, and the lights looked like they were all off in my unit. I waved to Harper and then turned to unlock my door. As the key clicked, the lights came on, and there was the sound of scrambling inside. I half expected to find Brandon with his latest flame, using the place as some kind of love den. But as I opened the door, I saw Jesse pulling his shirt back on.

My head turned towards the other person in the room. She had her back to me as she buttoned her shirt. Her chin-length brown hair was sticking out in all directions.

"Tay, I didn't think you'd be home tonight," Jesse breathed as he pushed his blond hair out of his grey eyes.

My mouth fell open, but I was too shocked to speak – too shocked that Brandon had been right about Jesse *having fun* so soon after Ashley.

I looked back to the girl and nearly choked as she turned.

"Amelia Saber?" I blinked. "Jess, what the hell?"

"You must be Taylor," Amelia said. I'd never met her before, but I'd seen her photos. I'd heard about her too, from Brandon who was dating her before he and Eden hooked up. No wonder Jesse hadn't told us about her.

"I'm Jesse's sister." I nodded. "And you're the mayor's daughter."

She smiled, but it didn't reach her eyes. It didn't even reach her cheeks. In fact, it looked incredibly melancholy.

"Sorry, you must get that a lot," I mumbled.

"Yes," she sighed. Her fingers tucked the front of her hair behind her ear, but it was too short to stay.

I scratched my chin and looked at my brother. He folded his arms.

"It's none of your business, Taylor," he said suddenly.

I blinked. "What?"

"Whatever you're thinking, stop. It's none of your business."

"I'm not thinking anything, except that I really need to study."

"Sure."

Amelia bit her lip. "I should go."

"No, stay," I replied. "I'm locking myself in my room anyway. Don't leave for my sake."

"No, I should go." She smiled, and it was a little less sad than before. She took a step towards Jesse, and then stopped and picked up her jacket from the floor. "It was nice to meet you, um, Taylor."

"You too, Amelia." I nodded. "Drive safe."

Her lips pressed together, and she slipped past me out the door. It swung shut, and I turned around.

"I don't want to hear it," Jesse mumbled. "Go and do your study."

"Jesse, talk to me," I sighed. "Quit shutting me out."

He exhaled. "I'm not shutting you out. I just don't feel the need to tell you every little thing about my life, okay?"

"Since when?"

"Since… since now, okay?"

"Not okay," I snapped. "Hey, what the hell is going on, Jess? What are you *doing* with Amelia Saber? You do remember that not so long ago that she and Brandon were seeing each other, right?"

He shrugged. "So?"

"So? Isn't there some kind of bro-code that you're breaking?"

"Since when do you care about Brandon?" he shouted. "Since when is this *any* of your business?"

"Jesse, I know that you're hurting, but—"

"Stop! You don't know anything about what I'm feeling!"

I gritted my teeth. "Because you won't *talk to me.*"

"Then take a hint."

I smacked the wall and felt it crumble beneath my palm. I stared at it, then my hand, and then looked at Jesse who didn't appear to be mad any more, just shocked.

"Are you all right?" he asked.

"Yeah," I sighed. "I… it must've been adrenaline or something."

Jesse shook his head and then lowered it.

I sat down. "Jesse, what are you doing with Amelia Saber?"

"Don't, Taylor. I'm not discussing this with you."

"If it's just fun, then you're doing it with the wrong girl," I murmured. "She's the mayor's daughter, she... she... Brandon really liked her, but she apparently liked someone else—"

He looked up. It was painted all over his face, the guilt, the grief, everything that he'd been keeping from me.

"No..." I breathed. "You?"

"I didn't cheat on... nothing happened before..." he replied. "But she may have broken up with Brandon because of me."

I rested my chin in my palms and covered my mouth. "Did she expect you to leave Ash—"

"No," he interrupted. "She just didn't want to be around me when I was with her."

"Jess, you're going to rip her heart out," I sighed. "It sounds like she really likes you."

He frowned. "What makes you think that I don't like her?"

"Do you?"

He blinked. "I... I don't know."

"Is that who you came back from Half Moon Bay to see?"

"I didn't come back to see anyone, I just couldn't be there with Brandon when he kept watching me, waiting for me to break – like you were here."

I exhaled. "We're just worried."

"I know, but it's hard enough being in this place after what happened without knowing that everyone is watching your every move," he said.

"Oh," I sighed. I hadn't thought of that. Ashley had died in here, and that alone would be a constant reminder to him every single day. I guess Eden was right, I was pretty selfish.

"I went out with a couple of guys that I went to uni with, and she was there with April," Jesse explained.

"My friend April?" I frowned. Old friend. "April McKenzie?"

He nodded. "Their brothers are friends or something. Anyway, Amelia had heard about what happened, I guess news travels fast around here."

"Six degrees of separation."

"More like three in South Coast."

I breathed a flat laugh. "Right."

Jesse shook his head. "We were just hanging out at first. She took my mind off it all, distracted me from everything. She didn't ask me about any of it, we just talked about random things. I do like her, Tay. I'm not playing her. That's not what it's about."

"Okay, I believe you." I nodded. "Why didn't you tell me any of this before?"

He shrugged and sat down beside me.

"So are you and her, like, together then?" I frowned.

"I don't know if I'm ready for that."

"Then what did I just walk in on?"

"If I said that we were just hanging out, would you believe me?"

I tipped my head. "If you said that you were just hanging out without shirts, then maybe."

109

He smiled weakly. Like Amelia's smile, it didn't reach his eyes, but it was a start.

"Jess, you're my brother, and I love you," I said. "I'm not here to judge, I'm not even here to speak if you don't want me to, but I am here."

He nodded. "I know. Thanks, sis."

I rested my head on his shoulder, and his hand found my knee.

"Hey, Tay?"

"Mm?"

"There's a hole in our wall from your hand."

I looked up. "Crap. Do you think that the bond will cover it?"

He glanced at me and let out a small laugh. "I'll swing by the hardware shop tomorrow and buy something to fill it."

"Probably a good idea."

He moved his hand to turn mine over. "It's not even red."

"Yeah, I'm a ninja."

He laughed again and although it sounded a little flatter than it used to, at least this time the smile reached his eyes.

*

From the moment that I got to the veterinary clinic at nine o'clock on Wednesday morning, I was run off my feet. I wasn't fully qualified yet, but I knew enough to help out. I was much better at the practical stuff than the theory. I knew what I needed to do; I just found it hard to put it into words sometimes.

"I'm just leaving now," I said to Harper on the phone after work. "How was your day?"

"*It was okay, long without you. How was yours?*"

"About the same. What are you up to now?"

"*I'm just checking in with Rob. He and Ebony asked me to stay for dinner,*" he replied. Rob was Eden and the twin's father, Joel's foster-father, and Harper's godfather. "*I can tell them no. I know that you wanted to watch a film and have our own dinner tonight.*"

"No, you stay with them. I'm sure they appreciate you being there," I sighed. "Plus, it's been a really long day, so I'm probably just going to try to get an early night."

"*Okay, if you're sure. I'll buy you lunch tomorrow to make up for it… and cook you dinner.*"

I smiled to myself. "I'm happy just to see you tomorrow. Tell Rob and Ebony I said hello."

"*Oui. Je t'aime.*"

"Love you too."

I hung up the phone and opened the door to my car. I dropped my bag on the seat, then checked underneath it. I'd found my kitten, Raven, under my car one of the last times I had finished late at the clinic. It was already going at seven o'clock. It had been a long day.

I arrived home to a dark house, only this time, as I unlocked the front door, there was no one scrambling for shirts and half-naked bodies waiting for me inside. Raven dashed passed me out the door as it creaked open. She moved quickly, like a dark blur at my feet. I reached in to flick the light on and dropped my bag inside the door before turning to look for her. Despite her size, she was still only a few months old so shouldn't be allowed outside yet. Outside was too dangerous for a young cat.

"Raven," I called. "Kitty."

I heard a hiss and hoped that she hadn't been bitten by something. There was the sound of a struggle, and I stopped to try and figure out where it was coming from. Raven gave another *meow*, and hiss, and I followed the sound around to inside the little courtyard area off my garage. On the other side of my bins, I found her.

The motion-sensor light came on as her paw swiped at something black.

I glanced at the bird, a raven, and frowned.

"Raven, no," I said. I picked up the kitten and blinked back at the black bird. Did it just flicker? Was it a supernatural raven?

I ran to take Raven inside, locking her in the small laundry, and then grabbed a towel and headed back out the front. I wrapped the towel around the bird, careful not to hurt its already wounded wing, and cradled it inside.

It didn't make any attempt to fly away, which was unusual for a wounded bird, but not unheard of. Maybe it was weaker than it looked, or perhaps, as the flicker would indicate, it wasn't really a bird.

I hooked the blanket from the back of the couch with my foot, and laid it on the cushion, then put the black raven down.

"Okay, you're safe," I sighed. I felt a little silly, considering I was still new at this, and there was a genuine possibility that I was just talking to a wounded bird.

I looked around the unit. Jesse must have been at work, or out with his new friend Amelia. Regardless, the coast was clear.

"We're alone," I said. "I—"

The raven made a strange low squawking sound and then began to shudder. The wings burst into fingers, and the body extended into human legs. I fell back on my elbows as a girl started to cough. I was glad that I'd wrapped the bird in the towel because she certainly didn't have feathers now to conceal her. She had lovely brown-satin skin, and black as black hair. Her eyes were the colour of midnight.

"Thank you for getting me out of the open," she croaked. I sat blinking and then moved forward to pass her the other blanket to cover herself.

"You... you're a person," I breathed. "Are you a shifter?"

Her head shook in quick movements. "No, a genie, or a *djinn*, whatever you would like to call me."

"So, why were you a raven and not like a ghostly spirit in a lamp?"

She tried to laugh, but it was weak. "I can pick my form. I like to fly."

I nodded.

"So, what are you?" she whispered. "A reaper or a banshee?"

"How did you know?"

"You've experienced death. I can see it in your eyes."

I frowned. "I'm a banshee. I can see your light. It's flickering. You're dying."

Her head shook. "Well, that's good news. As long as it's only flickering."

"What do you mean?"

"If it's flickering then it means that I may be hurt, but it's not quite my time to die. There's still hope."

"Hope?"

Her eyebrows drew. "You're new at this."

"Yes, I've only turned once."

"Very new." She exhaled. "Well, that's good, I guess. Experienced banshees might just scream at me here and now, and really make me glow."

I blinked. "I don't understand. I need a Full Moon."

"Bless, you are new." She coughed. She peeled back the towel from her right arm to reveal a scratch from her shoulder to her fingertips. It looked deep.

"Did my cat do that?" I gasped.

Her head shook. "No, another one, a panther."

"Panther... a black jaguar?"

"Yes, they are rare in South Coast outside of captivity."

I frowned. "I know one... knew one. I heard that she was back in town."

She exhaled deeply. "Perfect, a shifter. Do me a favour, banshee, heal me, and then I can run you through the basics."

"Heal you?" I blinked. "If you know anything about banshees, then you should know that I can't heal anyone. I've only ever hurt people."

Her head shook. "What's your name?"

"Taylor. Taylor Mistry."

"Taylor Mistry, put one of your hands on my head, and the other over my heart," she whispered. I hesitated but did as she said. When my skin made contact with hers, I gasped. I could feel the pulse of pain like a kind of heat in my fingertips. It didn't hurt me, but it was tangible. It was like touching a leather car seat that had been in the sun for a while.

"Now, Taylor Mistry, focus on what you feel. I bet it's a little warm," the girl said with a wry smile. "Try and make it cooler."

I swallowed. "How?"

"You're made up of silver, you're a conductor for heat and cold," she said in a breath. "Just focus."

I bit my lip and closed my eyes. I couldn't feel anything happening.

"Come on, Banshee. This is stage-one stuff. It should be a parlour trick for you."

"I've never done anything like—" my words cut off. Of course, of course I had. What else could explain what happened with Joel? His light changed when I was close to him. Had I healed him?

"Taylor," she whispered. "Help…"

Her dark eyes drooped closed. *No, no, no.* I took a deep breath and let it out. *Please don't die.*

I felt the warmth in her quivering body; I felt the coolness in mine. I focused on making them meet, on mixing them together. *Please don't die. I need to know more.*

The girl started choking, and I opened my eyes as she sat up. Her wounds had healed, but there was still a scar.

"Not bad." She coughed. "It'll work. Besides, scars are like battle wounds."

"I can't believe that worked." I blinked. "How did that work?"

115

The girl pulled the blankets around herself and sat up properly. "You did well, Baby Banshee."

I smiled. "Does healing work on everything?"

"No, only the supernatural beings who are not immortal. If they are immortal, then they can either heal themselves or crossover."

"So, it won't work on humans?"

"No," she answered. "You don't reap humans."

"Right." I nodded. "Sorry."

I don't know why I felt the need to apologise since being a banshee didn't exactly come with a manual.

"So, um, if you're a genie, then that means you're magic," I said. "Why didn't you just heal yourself?"

"That is too much personal gain," she sighed. "Got to read the fine print of the job description, it's a killer."

I breathed a laugh. "Literally."

She smiled. "Thank you, Taylor. You saved my life."

I honestly never thought that I'd ever hear anyone say that, never mind someone supernatural. In fact, I thought that I'd only hear the vow of revenge or the last intake of breath from supernatural beings.

"What's your name?" I asked.

She extended her unblemished hand. "Jenna."

"You're welcome, Jenna." I nodded, taking her hand to shake. "Thank you for teaching me that I could. I thought I could only bring death to things."

Her head tipped. "Who told you that?"

"Sal did. He's a reaper, a human reaper."

"Silly reaper. Banshees don't pick things to die, they don't target them. They're not hunters."

"I don't understand."

"Ever heard of the expression *'follow the light'* when people are dying? You are only following their light, helping them to crossover and move them on to their next life," she explained. "Banshees merely gravitate towards those who are dying or those who have given up and don't want to be here any more. Eternity is a long time, some cannot accept that fate."

I frowned. "But what about vampires? They live for an eternity, and they don't even have a glow."

"Vampires are undead immortals." She shrugged. "They have already experienced a kind of death. It's up to them to move themselves on. You only get one chance at an afterlife, they have already chosen theirs."

I covered my mouth. I couldn't believe what I was hearing. How had I gotten it all wrong? How had Sal gotten it all wrong? I wasn't a monster at all. I was a helper, a guide, a healer. But that didn't add up. Hunter didn't want to die, and I was sure that André didn't either, but I was drawn to them.

"Are you sure, Jenna? Because last Full Moon I think I killed someone who didn't want to die. In fact, it felt like I was after two shifters who didn't want to die."

She frowned. "I'm sure. I've known a few banshees over the years. It pays to know healers when I cannot heal myself."

"But that would mean that André wanted to die," I muttered. "And Hunter. That doesn't make sense, her light was bright too, but she didn't want to die. She was fighting me to stay alive."

"Well, from what I know of banshees, there was definitely something, a motive, that made the two of them *willing* to die. Only they could tell you what that reason was though."

I sat back. I was still trying to figure out what I was being told. I was still trying to connect what I had thought I knew with what I now know. I was trying to piece things together, to marry up the idea that banshees didn't bring harm to people. The one that I had known certainly wanted to bring harm to me.

"My boyfriend, Harper," I said. "He didn't want to die when I found him. He had been stabbed by a wolf-hunter."

"He's a wolf?" she asked. Her eyebrows lifted halfway to her hairline. "Odd couple. An animal with resistance to silver, and a girl entrenched with silver."

"We make it work."

She laughed. "Well, your boyfriend might not have wanted to die, but he was dying when you found him. Dying isn't always natural, it's not always a choice. Sometimes it's outside of your control. Did he die? Did you reap him?"

"No, I wasn't a banshee then. I was a human. I pulled the dagger out and ended up being marked... scratched by a banshee myself."

She folded her arms. "You were marked as a human? That's very rare."

"Yeah," I sighed. "She sent all sorts of creatures after me, then tried to kill Harper again on the next Full Moon. Can I get you some clothes?"

"I'm fine." She shrugged. She clicked her fingers and was suddenly robed in a lavish black feathery dress that covered the

118

scar down her right arm. The other was bare, but she still had the appearance of having wings even in human form. "You're wrong about that too, though."

"About what?"

"She didn't send creatures after you. Not consciously," Jenna replied. "If you were marked with death, then you were a natural magnet for the supernatural. They have a scent for those marked, it acts as a lure. Normally those that are marked will die because of their resistance to silver, but that's different in humans. If your boyfriend healed, and his light restored, unless he wanted to die, she wouldn't have come after him. She was probably after you since you were still alive and disturbed her work. You saw too much. I'm sure that your boyfriend and the shifter girl you know have told you about the importance of us all staying anonymous to humans. The humans who know too much are often collateral in our world."

"So you're saying that when I stopped to help Harper after he was stabbed, I was interfering?"

Jenna nodded. "I would say that when you stepped in, she was either about to ease Harper's suffering and heal him, as you healed me, or if it was his time and he wanted to depart, she would have taken his soul to the afterlife. Banshees don't just bring death, Taylor, they bring life. They mourn death with their cry; they feel the pain of those who fall."

"So how come I need to change at a Full Moon? I need to keep the balance of nature, right?"

She laughed. "I don't know who told you all of this nonsense. You change into the white woman to allow those who wish to die to pass through you. Any other day of the

Moon cycle, the spirits only pass on if they are killed. As a white woman, a banshee in true form, you are one of the crossroads between life and afterlife. The lights are the souls crying out for you, for death."

I tried to digest what I was hearing. "So banshees aren't evil?"

She smiled. "What is evil? There is no such thing. It is only fear and love that exist, not evil and good."

"Sure." I bit my lip. "So, why do I change back after reaping one person if not to maintain balance?"

"There must have been only one who was dying or willing to crossover."

"Oh, right. That makes sense."

Her head tipped. "I take it you killed the banshee who marked you?"

I frowned. "Not intentionally."

"Well, it was kill or be killed," she replied. "It sounds as though you have something to live for."

I nodded. "Wait, did you say that I mourn death by crying out? Like screaming? Is that why I've been doing that lately?"

"If you have been screaming, then yes. As I said, a banshee is a thoroughfare for supernatural spirits from this world into the afterlife."

"That makes sense," I sighed. "Harper and Cole thought as much, but—"

"Did you say Cole?" she asked. "Do you mean Cole Frost? The vampire?"

"Yes, do you know him?"

"I have heard of him. I have never met him before though."

"I'm sure that he'd be eager to meet you," I replied. "He's somewhat of a collector of the mystical."

"Indeed. So I've heard."

I pressed my lips together. "Well, I was just about to make some dinner. Are you hungry?"

She stood. "You have already shown me hospitality, Taylor Mistry. I won't overstay my welcome."

"You're very welcome to stay. My brother is out, and I always make too much," I said. "Besides, it's really lovely to talk to someone about this who actually knows what they're talking about. I have so many questions, and apparently, no one knows anything."

"Not even the illustrious Cole?"

I shook my head. "Not even him."

She thought for a moment. "Okay then, Taylor. I would love to stay for dinner."

It was interesting to talk to Jenna and hear about where she had travelled, and what she had seen. She told me that she was over eight hundred years old, and had been flying to wherever the wind had taken her since becoming a genie.

"The correct term for what I am is 'djinn', but I suppose I've commonly come to be known in English as a genie," she explained. "As I have already stated, as a djinn, I am able to transform into an animal of any description. I choose the raven, yes, because I like to fly, but it is also my spirit animal. The tribe that I came from must have looked upon the raven as their animal protector, as I can stay in the form longer than others."

"So how did you become what you are?" I asked. I had thrown together a chicken salad with whatever I had in the fridge. I hadn't gone grocery shopping in the last couple of days, but I made it a point to always have an abundance of vegetables at my disposal. They were the safest things to snack on.

"That I do not remember," she replied. "Though, mythology says that we are created from fire. I don't remember much about my human life, not my parents, or my friends. I only know of the raven as it is a form that comes naturally to me."

"I'm sorry, that must be hard not to know where you came from," I sighed. I joined her at the kitchen table and put down the plates. "Oh my gosh, I'm sorry. I hope chicken is okay. I didn't even think—"

"I'm not a real bird, Taylor, relax." She laughed. "It's wonderful. Thank you, no one has cooked for me for years."

I smiled and took a sip of my water.

"You haven't asked me the one thing that people normally lead with," she said. Her fork skewered some lettuce.

"I don't understand. I asked why you didn't live in a lamp, didn't I?"

She laughed. "Yes, I suppose you did. But that's not what I meant. I mean, what happens with the lamp. You didn't ask me whether I grant wishes."

"Oh."

I looked down at my salad and stabbed some food, shovelling it into my mouth. I chewed it a few times and then swallowed.

"So, do you grant wishes?" I asked.

"Not all djinns do it, or rather they avoid doing it by staying in animal form. In fact, most djinns are quite unfriendly."

"You don't seem unfriendly to me."

She glanced up and smiled. Her eyes were like black pearls. "I have my moments."

"Why is that? Why would they be unfriendly? Does it have something to do with the fact that you have to give people things when they don't necessarily deserve them?"

Jenna tipped her head. "What makes you ask that?"

I shrugged. "Aladdin. Jafar was a total jerk, and he got three wishes."

She laughed. "Yes, I suppose he was. You are very odd, Taylor Mistry."

"Thanks. Is it rewarding to give people what they want?"

"Granting wishes is difficult sometimes, Taylor," she sighed. "People aren't always happy with what they ask for."

"True."

She smiled. "Plus, in the recent past, people have not so much as asked for wishes, but rather taken or drawn on the magic from my kind. You would know them as magicians, or those who proclaim to be witches or warlocks."

"Magic?" I frowned. "Do you mean like Shadow Weavers and Light Lacers?"

"Now that is an interesting story."

123

"What do you mean?"

She sat back in her chair, and I did the same. I hadn't realised that my posture was so terrible as we were talking, but the topic made me want to whisper to keep the words as concealed as possible.

"Not many know the story of the origin of those two kinds. The two of them were born from a curse after being involved in a human feud of families in the battle for power," she explained. "The north of the Waning River, versus the south, or as it is commonly known, Iris Cove, versus the city of South Coast."

"Really? They originated here?"

"South Coast seems to be a magnet for supernatural beings."

I nodded. "So what happened?"

"As I said, the two groups were cursed. The northern people, Lucan Lacer's people became the Light Lacers. Iris is the Greek goddess of the rainbow, which is where the cove gets its name from. When light scatters, it makes rainbows. The Lacers all scattered upon being cursed. You won't find many of those around here anymore."

"I was told that Weavers were created to balance out the Lacers, is that not correct then?"

"No, you are correct. Lacers are the purer kind of magic. They are light magic, nature. They were the carers, the farmers."

"So why did they get cursed?" I asked.

"Because it was Lucan's wish to be successful in the nurturing of the land, but he and his people were cold and isolated." She smirked. "That is why Lacers make ice, though enjoy and gain power from the sun. It is a balancer."

"So what about the Shadow Weavers then? I was told that they weren't a natural breed of magic, and that a lot of them are trying to wipe-out the Lacers?"

"Ironic how that happened really," she mused. "Yes, they are a more artificial kind of magic. Shyam Weaver's people were warm and passionate people, dark-haired, as opposed to the Lacer fair-hair. The Weavers were the party animals. They stayed up all night and slept all day. Lunatics, they lived by moonlight, so hence draw their power from the Moon. Weavers are not born, because Shyam was a little kinder to his people in his wish. He requested that when they were ready for the power, that the next Blood Moon would grant their abilities. So as a result, they acquire them at different times according to that stipulation."

"Interesting," I sighed.

"You would know, Taylor, that both types also do not age," she continued. "The Lacers are frozen in early adulthood, while the Weaver's healing ability enables them eternal youth."

"Was that a part of the curse?"

She nodded. "The djinn who cursed them wanted to give them the chance of redemption, should they ever wish to return to humanity. As a means to prove their forgiveness to the other family, they were given the obstacle of nausea if they were near the other breed. If they could overcome their differences, then the spell would be reversed."

"But I know someone who is half-Lacer, half-Weaver. Cole said that his parents died from being near each other."

She shrugged. "Well, redemption is something that was never achieved, and cannot be achieved. It is a widely known fact that those who cross a djinn, even a friendly one, will live to regret it. Those associated with the two colonies continue to feel the force of the curse today as a result of their rebellion."

"Rebellion? What did they do to the djinn?" I frowned.

"Shyam and Lucan's people began to turn against the djinn for fating them all to the curse of magic. They didn't want to play nice with each other, but they wanted their way. The two of them returned to the djinn and sought mercy for their people; but the djinn did not grant their request, as their wish had already been made. In turn, they tried to destroy their creator, and so the chance at redemption was revoked as punishment."

"Why is it a bad thing to have magic?" I asked. "If they wanted the magic, and wanted the power if they asked for it, then why would they want to retaliate?"

"Because it was two selfish families that doomed an entire congregation of people… people that were not all happy with the change. The thing that you need to remember, Taylor, is that not everyone knows what they really want, so when they are positioned with wishes, they make the wrong ones or are not clear on what they ask for. The Lacer family wanted the means to make crops flourish, and live off the land. They wanted to grow plants with their hands, and get around paddocks as quickly as possible. They wanted to make people sleep with a touch so they would not be kept up all night. The Lacer family spoke on behalf of a whole people, and djinns cannot do anything but grant their wish. The Weavers heard of this, they heard of their powers, and so found the same djinn and asked for their own collection of abilities. Being more reckless to their opposing, they wanted to manipulate objects, and the power of invisibility, they wanted to freeze time, and poison by contact to ruin the crops. The Weavers doomed their own settlement to ensure that they were not outnumbered. It was selfish, but again, the djinn could not refuse the request. Lacers and Weavers cannot heal from each other's magic because they originate from the same branch. That is why they are compatible to a degree. That is why you know a mixed breed Light Weaver, though they are very rare."

I sat silent for a moment, letting the story sink in. It was difficult to grasp that it was such a small thing that had happened, but it actually affected a number of people... people that I know today.

"Can the curse ever be lifted?" I asked. "What happens if the djinn who granted their wish dies? Will it break?"

"No," she whispered. "Once the magic of a djinn is concocted, it is intact. The curse will never be broken, because a djinn cannot interfere with another's magic, nor can the original djinn retract it."

"Everything has consequences," I murmured.

"Yes."

I bit my lip and glanced at my almost untouched salad. I was glad that it had started off cold because a hot meal would be almost inedible by now.

"How do you know so much about them?" I asked. "You said that not many know the story of their origin."

"Yes." She smiled. "I know the story because I was the djinn who cursed them. As I said before, Taylor Mistry, I may seem friendly, but I have my moments."

Jenna glanced back to her salad and pierced another forkful that she gracefully scooped into her mouth.

I felt jarred by the revelation – by the powerful genie sitting before me. I didn't quite know what to do with the knowledge.

"Relax, Taylor," she sighed. "I will not harm you. I do not use magic on those who do not ask for it."

I let my shoulders drop. "Sorry, it's just a lot to take in."

"Understandable." She nodded. "This is a delicious meal. Thank you once again for your hospitality."

I breathed a laugh. "I'm always happy to show kindness to the most powerful supernatural being on the planet."

"Perhaps, but you could still reap me."

I dropped my fork. "What?"

"Life is a balancer, Taylor Mistry. No one has the right to live forever."

Her words made me shiver, though I wasn't cold. I turned my attention back to my food.

"There is one thing that I'm still curious about," I said.

"Sure," she replied.

"Recently, Harper, my—"

"Your werewolf boyfriend, yes."

I smiled. "Right, well, he had a flicker in his light. It was there for a while, but when he was stabbed with a dagger, a hunter's dagger, and healed, the flicker disappeared."

"Your boyfriend doesn't have much luck with hunter's daggers, does he?"

"I guess not."

Jenna pressed her plump brown lips together. "Well, perhaps the wound prompted something in him to heal what he couldn't heal before. Were you with him?"

"Yes, I sat with him afterwards."

She nodded. "Well, maybe it was you who healed him in some way. Or maybe he was just more efficient in healing himself since his body has clearly been in overdrive with all the stabbings."

I looked down. "So it's not possible that he can live forever?"

"No one lives forever, Taylor. Not really. There comes the point where everything must end."

I rubbed my forehead. "So… why is his glow dim again?"

"It is simply not his time to die. He is obviously in fine health."

"But it looks almost the same as the vampires. He looks immortal."

"All healthy supernatural beings who are not in danger of dying look like that, Taylor," she replied. "Perhaps you just haven't seen enough of a variety to know. It is the same for human reapers, those who are healthy, and have a lot of time left, do not look dark to them. Light until the darkness falls, as opposed to what you see, dark until the light rises."

I nodded.

We ate in silence for a few more moments, and then Jenna put her fork down. She took a sip of water and sat back. I poked my last piece of lettuce into my mouth.

"Well, Taylor Mistry, that was exquisite." She smiled. "Thank you once again for your kindness."

I nodded. "You're welcome, anytime. Like I said, I've enjoyed the company."

"Me too actually."

"You sound surprised."

"I suppose I am a little," she replied. "But I must admit that, although your kitten was trying to make me her plaything, I'm glad that it was your courtyard I fell into."

"Raven. My kitten's name is Raven."

"Appropriate."

I nodded. "So, I have a feeling that in a few seconds you're going to say that you need to leave. I just wanted to tell you that, even though I have uni tomorrow, there's a strong possibility that I'll be going to visit Cole afterwards. If you want me to introduce you to him, then you can either meet me here or… or at uni, or something."

She smiled. "Thank you, Taylor. I would like that. As long as I won't be intruding."

"I'll call and ask first if you like." I shrugged. "He is kind of private."

"Well, we can otherwise meet on mutual ground if it is preferred."

"Maybe the cemetery? That's mutual, and people don't stay there for long periods."

She laughed. "That is okay by me. Why don't I meet you at your uni? I'm between phones."

"SCU common room at two-thirty then?"

"Sure."

Jenna stood up and smoothed her feathery skirt. "Once again, Taylor, it's been a pleasure."

I stumbled to my feet. "Oh, um, me too. Really, thank you for sharing your knowledge with me. You are so amazing."

Her head lowered in a polite nod. "Do you have any more burning questions before I leave?"

"Just one," I whispered. It had been one that I'd wanted to ask her all evening. I didn't know why I was so nervous to ask it. Prolonging the question didn't make the answer change. It was yes or no, true or false.

"What is it, Taylor?" she asked.

I swallowed. "Do banshees age? I mean, will I be like this until I... I die?"

She smiled a sad smile. "Nothing lasts forever."

"But... but what does that mean exactly?"

"It means that you will age, but you may not live as long as a human would. There always needs to be someone at the crossroads."

I frowned. "So I'll die young? How long is *not as long*?"

She walked over and picked up the ends of my hair. I looked down at her thumb as it brushed them.

"You will probably never need to worry about grey hair."

It was hard to hear, but maybe harder not to know. I think.

"Make the most of your life, Taylor Mistry. You are one of the lucky ones that got a second chance at it."

131

She lifted her scarred hand to my cheeks, then turned to leave. As her feathers fluttered out the door, her words finally sank in.

Kill or be killed.

Becoming a banshee saved my life. It was my life now. Without it, without any of it, Harper might have died, but I would have lived on as normal. With it, I could... I would live, just not as long.

I looked down at my hands, turning them over and over until they formed fists that made my silver-embedded nails tear into my palms.

My life or his, it had always come down to my life or his.

I wouldn't have changed a thing.

Phase Five
The Ties of Friendship

I picked at the plastic wrap from my sandwich at two o'clock as I waited in the common room for Jenna. I'd tried to do some work in the library after class, but my mind wasn't in it. It was drifting in and out of Jenna's words from the night before.

"It is a mystery as to why you spend so much time here, Taylor Mistry," a sarcastic voice said.

I looked up. "Oh. Hey, Sal."

"Hey?" He frowned. "*Hey?* Taylor Mistry, I am disappointed. No witty *you're ridiculous, Salvatore?*"

"You know that you are," I sighed.

"Everything good?"

I nodded. "I'm just waiting for a friend."

"What friend? Aren't I your only friend?"

"No."

"Ouch," he groaned. He sank into the bench beside me. "Who's your friend?"

"Her name is Jenna."

He frowned. "Interesting. A girl."

"Why is that interesting?"

"You just seem to have more male friends than female friends. Actually, considering your only female friend is a vampire, and technically dead, I'm not even sure it counts."

I pressed my lips together.

"Seriously, what is with you today?" he asked. "Did something happen?"

"Can I ask you something, Sal?"

"Do you think that I'd say no?"

I rolled my eyes. "Had you seen me before that first time we met in the library?"

"I believe it was outside the library that we technically met," he replied.

"Whatever, same thing," I said with a groan. "Had you seen me before then?"

"What do you mean?"

"Had you ever visited me as a job? A reaping job, I mean."

He scratched his head. "Where's this coming from?"

"Well, I was marked with death for a while, and I know that I came pretty close to it on a few occasions," I said. "I was still human, even with the mark, so that would have fallen under your jurisdiction."

Sal exhaled. It was as good as a resounding *yes*.

"You did," I whispered. "That's why you were staring at me strangely, and how come you knew that I was different."

"Taylor, I knew that you were different just by looking at you. I told you that I read vibes, and yours was no longer a human one."

"When did you visit me?" I asked. "When was I going to die?"

"Taylor," he sighed, and adjusted his sitting position. I hadn't ever seen him this uncomfortable before.

"Please?"

His eyes lifted to find mine. "I was called to you four times. The first was when it was stormy, and the branch hit you. As soon as Harper showed up, I was no longer needed. The second was when you had the snakebite, and were in the black Jag at the cemetery. Nice first aid issued by Doctor Frost there though. The third was when you were running through the woods, though it was only for a glimmer before I was no longer needed."

I nodded. I had been running from the wendigo, and Cole and Harper had come to my rescue. Apparently, as soon as the threat of death was overturned, the presence of a reaper was unnecessary.

"And the fourth?"

He rubbed his black brow. "Taylor, I really don't think—"

"Tell me, Salvatore."

He sighed. "The wolf. In the cabin."

"Harper."

He nodded. "I didn't know that it was him at the time, but after I met you both and figured out what he was, then it made sense."

"He was going to kill me," I murmured. "But he didn't."

I forced myself to think back to the unpleasant moment when the Full Moon had forced Harper into wolf form. I remembered that his razor-sharp teeth were millimetres from me. I remembered pleading that he made my death quick. Tears prickled in my eyes as I remembered *why* he hadn't killed me then and there. The dagger, the flash of white. He'd wanted me to kill him instead, but I couldn't do it. He'd lost his footing on the floorboards, scratches that were still deep-set in the wood to this day. The banshee that I'd replaced had come in, the white woman, the waif. She had hypnotised me, presumably before attempting to kill me, but was intercepted by Harper, and sank her fingers into his shoulders in the same place where mine had recently punctured him. I fought back. I won. I was changed forever.

"He was going to kill you, Taylor," Sal whispered. "I was there. I was there until she grabbed him, so I was surprised to learn that he survived."

"You left after that? After she attacked Harper?"

He nodded. "You weren't in danger any more. The threat was eliminated."

"But what about the banshee? She was going to kill me. Kill or be killed, right?"

"I don't know about that, I just know that as soon as the wolf was put down, I was no longer needed because you were safe. Who knows if I would have needed to come back after he died."

"Banshees don't kill unless supernatural beings want to die, or are being killed," I mumbled, mostly to myself. "I was never going to kill him. Does that mean that Harper wanted to die?"

"Hm? What's that?"

"Banshees take any supernatural souls that want to crossover on the Full Moon and then turn back human," I said. "I took André last Full Moon, and then changed back. You left after she went after Harper because I was no longer in danger.

Maybe she was never going to kill me. Maybe she was just there because Harper wanted to die rather than hurt me. For all we know, she would have changed back human and ended up where she had come from."

"You've lost me, Mistry."

"But then, if I didn't kill her, Harper would have died that night. As it was, he nearly did."

Sal blinked. "But you killed his reaper."

"Right." I nodded. "I did. I killed his reaper, then became one."

"Poetic."

I glared at him, and then glanced up as Jenna walked through the door. Her feathery dress was shorter today, but still covered the scar down her right arm that had been left by the previous night's wounds.

"You made it." I smiled.

"Of course." She nodded. Her eyes traced to Sal. "Well, which one is this?"

Sal looked up at her and blinked.

Jenna smiled. "Ah, the reaper."

He frowned. "You're not human."

"Sal. Salvatore Vincent, this is Jenna," I said.

"Pleasure," Jenna replied.

"Charmed." Sal nodded. He looked back to me. "Mistry, this isn't a human female friend."

I exhaled. "I said that her name is Jenna, not that she was human."

"Technicalities, Taylor Maye, you scientist, you. So what type of friend is she then, apart from a not human and female one?"

"A supernatural one." I shrugged. "One that knows more than you."

He pulled a face. "Cole knows more than me."

"But she knows more about banshees than him."

Jenna sighed. "I'm a djinn."

Sal's orange eyes popped. "You got yourself a genie friend? Taylor Maye Mistry, I am so impressed."

I pushed him in the face, and he made a grumbling sound.

"So, what do you know?" Sal asked. "Did you find out what the screaming is all about?"

I folded my arms. "Well, as Cole and Harper assumed, it's for the supernatural deaths."

He nodded and turned to Jenna. "Huh. So why does it happen less often for her than it does for me?"

"Silly reaper." Jenna huffed. She flicked her finger at Sal, and his nose twitched.

"Ouch, hey, watch it, Djinn." He groaned.

"It's Jenna."

"Whatever."

Jenna's eyebrow lifted. "What do you think, Grim? Supernatural beings are more durable than human beings. Naturally, they die less often."

"Ah, true." He nodded. "And if you're going to call me by my occupation, don't call me *Grim*. I'm a reaper, not a grim."

I rolled my eyes. Sal had told me once that he didn't like the fact that people assumed that death is grim, so added *grim* to his *reaper* title. He'd made the point that death wasn't always glamorous, but it didn't have to be horrible or bleak either.

"That is a fine point," Jenna replied. "It's always nice to hear of someone who enjoys their job."

Sal's head tipped. "I wouldn't go that far. I'm not a masochist."

She laughed. "I like this one."

"You'd be the only one," I mumbled.

"Ouch, Mistry, very ouch," Sal sighed theatrically. "So where are you two headed?"

"The cemetery," I said. "Cole is looking forward to meeting you, Jenna."

Sal pulled a face. "In the cemetery? Mistry, you give reapers a bad name with all the hanging out there that you do."

I shrugged. "It's a safe place for me."

"You need to get out more."

"I get out plenty."

"Shall we go, or would you two like to find a bathroom to burn off the tension?" Jenna asked.

"I have a boyfriend," I said at the same time Sal said. "*She has a boyfriend.*"

Jenna nodded, but seemed sceptical.

I pushed Sal in the face again, and he grabbed my wrist.

"Quit it, Banshee, or I'll scream," he said in a muffled voice.

I laughed and stood up, but Sal didn't let go of me.

"Is Wolfie coming?"

"He's coming with Cole and Ruby." I nodded. "Why?"

"I'm coming too."

I groaned. "Sal."

"Mistry," he sighed. "Taylor, please."

"Bring the reaper," Jenna said. "It's okay with me."

Sal released my hand, and I walked around to where Jenna stood. She reached out and squeezed my arm in a comforting gesture, and I led the two of them out to where I'd parked my car.

"You know, a reaper and a banshee is probably the smartest cross-species match there is," Jenna said as I unlocked the doors.

"Huh?" I frowned. I nearly stumbled in behind the steering wheel. "Why?"

"Well, because a banshee cannot reap a reaper."

"I told you, Taylor Mistry." Sal grinned.

I rolled my eyes. "You also told me that banshees hunted supernatural creatures for a sport."

Jenna shook her head. "Silly reaper."

I turned to glare at him, and he shrugged.

"Alba told me she could hunt them," he replied.

"Maybe because she wanted to hunt *you*," I said. Sal pulled a face at me and then I glanced back to Jenna. "So it is true that I can't reap Sal then?"

"What reason do I have to lie?" Jenna shrugged. "Reapers only become what they are as they are humans who made a bargain with death. Sal traded his human life for a life as a reaper, so the former could die. When he is done with his life, then he will trade places with someone dying and will pass on naturally himself. Life is circular."

"Thank you, Elton John," Sal muttered.

I fought against a smile, but Jenna looked confused by the reference. Sal grinned at me, and I rolled my eyes, pulling into the one-way street.

Sal or Jenna didn't speak at all for the remainder of our journey to the cemetery, so we drove in silence. Sal's gaze switched between looking out the back window and looking into the rear vision mirror at me. Jenna just glanced curiously around the car.

When we arrived at the cemetery, I parked in the external car park and turned off the engine.

"We'll walk the rest of the way, it's not far," I said.

"Amund Tomb?" Sal asked. He had been there once before when I was there – on the last Full Moon and the first night that I had turned into the white woman.

"Near there."

"I knew the Amund family. They werewolf-hunters," Jenna said. "Did you know that Amund means divine protection in Scandinavian?"

Sal laughed. "Seriously? Well, that's outstandingly ironic."

"Why?"

"Because wolf-hunters have been nothing but trouble for Taylor, so the fact that she finds refuge in their tomb is…yeah, hm, ironic."

"Great," I sighed. "Let's go."

"How did they die?" Sal asked.

I stomped off down the bitumen road of the cemetery towards the tomb.

"They died as their name implied," Jenna answered. "Protecting."

"By a wolf?" Sal pressed.

I turned around. "Salvatore, seriously, stop talking."

Sal recoiled. "Why? I'm just curious."

"Just don't be. I don't want to hear any more about death."

"Taylor, we're in a cemetery."

I blinked and then turned back to continue down the road. I didn't want to think about how soon or otherwise that I'd be joining the residence here. I didn't want to consider that in some other turn of fate, I might otherwise have ended up like the Amund family, murdered while trying to protect – even if I had been trying to protect the wolf and not reap it.

They saw me before I saw them, so Harper began walking towards us. I started to jog and felt my chest tighten. I really regretted letting my fitness go by the wayside after it had once saved my life – even Sal had confirmed that.

I threw my arms around Harper as we met and squeezed him tight. I hadn't seen him in over a day, which was long for us. Plus, considering all that I'd learnt recently, my days were relatively numbered, so I wasn't too keen on wasting them.

"What a nice hello," Harper murmured. He pressed his lips to my throat, and I ran my fingers down the side of his face to lift his eyes to mine. They were big, and clear olive-green, and twinkling in the sun. They were my favourite colour. They narrowed in confusion.

"Is something wrong?" he asked.

"No, nothing. Nothing now," I replied.

"I'm sorry I missed your lunch break."

"That's okay, I only had a few minutes," I sighed. I wrapped my arms around his shoulders again and saw that Cole was standing behind him. He wasn't with Ruby as I thought he would be, but he wasn't alone. Lesleigh was with him.

"Where's Ruby?" I asked.

"She was needed elsewhere," Harper replied. "Lesleigh was eager to come and meet—"

"Hello." Jenna smiled. "You must be Harper. My name is Jenna."

Harper nodded. "Jenna. It's a pleasure to meet you. Taylor has been singing your praises."

"At least she's not screaming them."

Sal laughed from behind her, and we all turned to stare at him. He shook his head as his dumb smile faded.

"Grim, you made it. I wasn't aware that you were invited," Harper said flatly.

"And miss out on an opportunity to hang out with my favourite wolf? Unlikely."

I exhaled. "Come on, Jenna, come and meet Cole."

Her dark eyes shone with their own backlight as they lifted towards the pale, blond vampire. Cole looked up from his pacing and began walking towards us. His hands stayed in his pockets until he was a couple of steps away. He lifted his right hand towards her.

"Jenna, I presume," he said. "Thank you for agreeing to meet with me."

"Cole Frost, your reputation precedes you. The pleasure is all mine."

He smiled, and his dimples seemed to gleam in the sunlight. "Is it your first time in South Coast?"

"Not at all, I am very familiar with the place's history. Including your part in it, Nicolas. Nicolas Harrison Frost."

The smile on Cole's face faded. "Indeed, it seems that I underestimated just how much my reputation precedes me."

"Don't worry, your secret is safe," Jenna said with a wink. "We're all friends here, after all."

"Hello, Jenna," Lesleigh said. "It's been a long time."

"Lesleigh Ramon, you stopped aging."

"It's Lesleigh White now."

Jenna's dark brow lifted. "You were married?"

"Fleetingly."

The boys and I exchanged confused expressions.

"Leigh, when did you know Jenna?" Cole asked. We all glanced at the brunette vampire. She looked again as if she had just stepped off a runway in her fitted three-piece suit.

Lesleigh's silver eyes rolled. "Cole, darling, you know that I spent time here in my adolescence between Spain and Manchester. Jenna has been around for years, and I met her in my travels."

Cole nodded. "As a human."

"Of course as a human, I have not gone by the name Ramon in years and years."

Jenna nodded then stepped forward to embrace the vampire.

"You have not changed a bit, Jenna," Lesleigh noted. "Although, my memory of you is a little fuzzy."

"But you do remember me."

"I never forget a raven."

"Indeed."

I felt as though my steam had been snuffed. Lesleigh clearly knew the genie better than me. It was a wonder that she and Cole had never been introduced.

"I did not expect to find you with Mister Frost," Jenna said.

"Doctor," Lesleigh corrected. "And I am not *with* Cole, we are very old friends. I took him under my wing when he was turned."

Cole huffed, and Lesleigh nudged him. They really did act like siblings rather than old friends.

"Well then, are we going to stay in this drab setting, or shall we go somewhere a little more appropriate?" Lesleigh asked. "I do rather despise cemeteries. They're so... concrete."

"Oh, I just wasn't sure if—" I started.

"It's quite all right, Taylor, you made the right call in regards to choosing a mutual place for an introduction." Cole smiled. "We can all go to Crescent, if you prefer. It doesn't open for a few hours, and Ruby is doing some work there."

"I'm not... I don't... you don't need me to come," I replied. I wasn't a big fan of bars, even closed bars. As much as I wanted to learn more from Jenna about banshees, I had a feeling that today wasn't about me.

"What do you mean?" Jenna asked. "Don't you want to come?"

"You and Lesleigh clearly have some catching up to do, and I'm sure that Cole has a lot of questions for you." I shrugged. "We can meet up another time. If... if you like."

145

Jenna smiled. "Of course, Taylor. I would love that."

Sal sighed.

"What?" I frowned.

"Nothing."

Harper curled his hand around mine and squeezed it. "I'll take you home then."

I smiled at him. "Why don't I meet you there? I need to take Sal back. Unless you'd like to go to Crescent with them, Sal?"

"No, I'm good," Sal replied. "Let's go, Mistry."

"We can take him back, Taylor, if you would like to go with Harper," Cole offered. "Crescent is near SCU."

Sal's face looked pained. It made me laugh.

"It's fine, I can take him," I said. "It's no trouble, really."

Sal relaxed.

"Well, I'll come with you. Cole drove me, so I don't have a ride anyway," Harper said.

Sal rolled his orange eyes.

"Okay, well let's go," I sighed. "See you later, Jenna. Cole, Lesleigh."

"Take care, Taylor." Jenna nodded.

Cole and Lesleigh waved.

I led the two boys back to my car, and Harper opened my door for me. I heard Sal groan as I slipped in the passenger seat.

"Something on your mind, Grim?" Harper asked, although his tone suggested that he wasn't particularly interested in what it was. He sat in the driver's seat as Sal took his place in the back.

"Nope," Sal mumbled. "I just don't know why Taylor isn't capable of opening her own doors, or driving for that matter."

"It's called chivalry."

"It's called being controlling is what it is."

"Sal, just drop it," I sighed. "I don't mind."

Harper glanced at me. "Would you prefer to drive?"

"No, it's fine really," I replied.

Sal leant forward from the back seat. "You know, open communication is rule number one in relationships."

"Salvatore, shut it or you're walking home," I snapped. "Besides, when's the last time you were in a relationship?"

Sal sat back and folded his arms. He didn't reply, and I could see from his expression that I'd hit a nerve.

"Sorry," I breathed. "I didn't mean—"

"Yeah, you did," he mumbled. "Can you just drive already, Wolfie? I have stuff to do."

Harper started the car, and I bit my lip. For the second time in a lifetime, Sal was silent as we drove all the way back to SCU. It ate away at me that I had offended him, even if my initial intention was to shut him up.

Harper pulled into a carpark by the student housing, and Sal was opening the door before the handbrake was on.

"Thanks," Sal said, sliding out of the car.

"Wait, Sal," I called. I looked back to Harper. "I'll be just a second."

Harper frowned but nodded. I made a mental note to ask him about his sulking later.

"Sal, hey, wait up," I yelled. He was already halfway through the door that led to the stairwell to his dorm.

"Save it, Mistry," he grumbled.

"I'm not leaving until you talk to me."

He stopped on the top step. "About what? What have I done this time?"

"Nothing, this one's on me."

He waited.

I bit my lip. "I'm sorry about what I said before."

"Okay."

"Is it?"

"Sure." He shrugged. "It was probably my fault anyway. I shouldn't have made the comment about Harper doing that stuff for you."

"You just called him Harper."

"That is his name, right?"

I rolled my eyes. "Yes. So are we okay?"

"Yes, Taylor Maye Mistry, we're fine." He smiled.

I turned and took a step down. "Just out of curiosity, why don't you have a girlfriend? I mean, you can be annoying sometimes but, other times, you can be really sweet."

His eyebrows lifted. "Sweet?"

"Or whatever."

He chuckled. "Stop, you're making me blush."

"But seriously."

"Seriously." He smirked. "My last girlfriend got mad that I kept disappearing at inappropriate times without a good reason. The one before that turned into a job. I figured I'd save myself the inevitable heartache."

"But—" I started. My words cut off as a door opened and someone walked past us down the stairs.

Sal pressed his lips together. "But?"

"But what about someone…" I stopped and leant in. "Not human?"

Sal laughed. "They're harder to find than you think."

"I know a few."

"In relationships."

"Eden's not any more, and I could ask Jenna if she's—"

"Taylor, just leave it. I'm not interested in them," he sighed. "Go back to your boyfriend. He's probably getting impatient."

I nodded and turned to leave. When I had reached the door, I looked back up at him and found him still in the same spot.

"Lunch tomorrow?" I asked. "I have a class until one thirty, but I could meet you afterwards if you want?"

"Sure," he sighed. "I'll see you then."

I waved and slipped out, jogging back to where Harper was waiting. He'd turned off the engine in my absence. He didn't speak as I climbed back in, but silently started the car and shifted into reverse.

"I'm sorry," I murmured.

He glanced over at me. "What for?"

"For keeping you waiting." I shrugged. "For whatever I've done to upset you."

"I'm not upset, Taylor."

"You're not?"

"I just… I just think the grim was clearly attention seeking before. He wanted your attention, and you fell for it," Harper said.

"Fell for it?" I frowned. "Sal was upset about what I said. I wanted to make it right."

"Why?"

"Because I shouldn't have said it."

Harper lifted his shoulders. "You didn't say anything too bad. You made a good point actually."

"Regardless," I sighed.

We continued driving in charged silence. I could feel my heart thumping against my ribcage, and it was making my entire body shudder. I didn't like that Harper was upset with me when I was only trying to do the right thing by my friend. I wished that I could take it all back and just keep my mouth shut to begin with.

"Harper, please don't be mad at me," I mumbled.

He slowed in front of my unit and put my car in park. I unclipped my seat belt.

"I'm not mad," he replied. "I'm just confused."

"Why?" I frowned. "What about?"

"About why you still spend time with the grim when he is not useful to you any more."

"It's not about being useful, he's a friend." I shrugged. "I just think he misses my company."

Harper lifted his eyebrows. "He misses you, Taylor. He misses you needing him."

"What? No, we're just friends."

"Taylor, do not tell me that you don't see it," he sighed. "The guy flirts with you all the time. It's a little embarrassing."

I breathed a laugh. "What are you talking about?"

"I can't blame him, but I just wish that you wouldn't encourage him the way that you do."

"What? No, I don't, Harper."

His head tipped. "You have lunch dates with him."

"I've had one… and it wasn't a date."

Harper sighed. "Okay."

"Where is this even coming from? Have I ever given you the impression that I want to be with him and not you?"

"No." He frowned. He dropped his head and stared at his palms. "But it's coming from the place inside me that knows he's better for you."

"What?" I asked, and tried not to think of what Jenna had said in the car earlier. "Don't be ridiculous."

Harper looked up at me. "He is, Taylor, he's better suited to you than I am. Think about it. Out of me, the grim, and even the wolf-hunter, I am the only one that is bad for you. The others you match up with in some way or another, you're equals. You are a supernatural reaper and a supernatural hunter. I am just supernatural."

"I'm not a hunter, we were wrong about that," I said. "On the Full Moon, I only reap those who are dying or want to pass on. I don't hunt; I just follow their lights and help the souls crossover."

Harper nodded. "Okay, so it's just him then. The reaper – just like you."

"I don't want him, I want you," I answered. "You *know* that I only want you. I can be friends with him and be in love with you at the same time."

"Maybe. Maybe you can," he murmured. "But he is attracted to you, whether you want to admit it or not."

"Do you not trust me?"

He shook his head. "Taylor, of course I trust you."

"Well, that's what it comes down to." I shrugged. "Harper, I didn't want to bring this up, but bear in mind that you still frequently see one of the girls that you used to sleep with, and who is actually still in love with you. I trust you to be around her."

"You mean Hunter?" He frowned. "The friend that I haven't seen since she stabbed me and tried to kill you?"

I dropped my face into my hands and rubbed my eyes. "Why are we even having this conversation? It's so stupid."

"I'm sorry. I'm sorry that I brought it up," Harper whispered.

I looked up. "No, if it's bothering you, then fine. But I just don't understand *why* it bothers you."

"Because you love me," he breathed. "But you run after him."

I blinked back tears. "I didn't run *after* him. I was apologising to him for being rude. I would run after you every time, Harper. *Every* time."

"Okay."

His head dropped back down, and I stared at him, waiting for him to say more. At least when he was talking, I could try to placate his toxic thoughts. When he was silent, I felt like I was suffocating.

"Harper," I whispered.

He looked up and instantly crumbled when he saw my face.

"Taylor…" he sighed. "Taylor."

He moved to unclip his seatbelt and then leant over to capture my lips with his. He moved his hand over my wet cheek and then dropped it to my waist, turning me towards him. I climbed over the middle console to sit on his lap, but my back pushed against the car horn and it scared the life out of both of us.

I moved forward against him. "It's a little too squishy here. Let's go inside."

Harper nodded, reaching up to tuck my messy hair behind my ear. His hand settled on the side of my face as he brushed my cheek.

"I'm sorry. I'm sorry that I let my jealousy get the better of me," he whispered. "I'm sorry that I upset you."

"I'm sorry that I gave you any reason to be jealous." I replied as I ran my finger over his lips. "I never want you to think that I want to be with anyone else, regardless of how better suited or whatever they are. I love you, Harper Lovett, even if we're perfectly imperfect together."

"Perfectly imperfect," he breathed, and a smile hung from the corner of his lips.

My hand fell to the neck of his T-shirt. "I like this on you."

"What? My T-shirt?"

I nodded. "But I think it'll look better on my floor."

He chuckled. "I tend to agree."

*

I tapped my pen against my page while Harper ran his fingers down my back. It was distracting, but I needed to get my uni work done. I was in the second week of the three-week winter term, and my exam was in two weeks. I was looking forward to that as much as I was the Full Moon that fell on the Sunday of exam week.

"Harper," I sighed.

"Mm?"

"This is important."

He laughed. "So is this."

"I could fail again."

"I would pass you."

I turned to look at him. "I need more than a pass to keep studying what I'm studying."

"If we need to be awake this early, we might as well enjoy it." Harper smiled and flopped back against my pillows. The sight of him in all his shirtless glory made me begin to question my own sanity. I shook my head to clear it.

"No, I need to finish this, so stop being all Harper-like. It's distracting."

He laughed. "I don't know what you mean."

"You know exactly the kind of effect that you have on me when you look at me with those puppy-dog eyes."

"No, tell me," he said as he scooped me up in his arms. I yelped as my blanket slipped, and I tucked it back around me. Harper brushed my hair over my shoulder. "You have an effect on me too, you know."

"Preposterous," I whispered.

"Fact."

"I wish that I could understand it, but I don't. I don't understand why you feel jealous over me or why you want to risk your life—"

"I'm not risking anything," he answered. "Nothing not worth the risk."

I ran my fingers over his arms that were securely around me, drawing the patterns in the scars that my nails had caused.

"For such a logical person, I don't understand how you could say that being with me is worth more than your life," I replied.

His eyebrows lifted. "Love is always worth more than life. It transcends it. You have already put your life on the line for me more than once."

"That's different."

"How?"

"You… you're…"

I wanted to tell him that he couldn't protect me from what I would inevitably face and that he would probably out-live me. I wanted to tell him that saving him was my greatest achievement, and just being with him was more than I could ever ask for in a lifetime. But I couldn't. If this problem were shared then, it would be a problem doubled. He didn't need this guilt. He had taken on enough of it from my oversights.

"I am what?" he asked. "Whatever you are going to say is completely without principle."

"You're worth saving," I amended. "That's all I was going to say."

He ran his hands through my hair, forcing my head back. "Well, I happen to think that you are too."

"You can't save me from everything."

He tipped my head back straight, and confusion swam in his eyes. "I can try."

I looked away, and Harper's hand moved to rest on my chest.

"Your heart is beating fast," he murmured.

"I'm just worried about you."

"Why? Jenna said that banshees don't hunt, so I am safe as long as I do not will death upon me."

"Unless something else happens to you… like a wolf-hunter."

His head tipped contemplatively.

"You know, Jenna told me a lot of things about what I am. She knows a lot about a lot of things," I whispered. "Do you think that they're all true?"

"Cole said that djinns are demi-gods. She has no reason to lie to us."

I nodded.

"Why? What did she say?" he asked. "You haven't yet had the chance to tell me."

"She cleared up some things that Sal had wrong." I shrugged. "The hunting thing mostly, and confirmed what you and Cole thought that the cries were about. Banshees mourn the supernatural dead; they are at the crossroads between life and the afterlife." I looked down at my hands as they ran over his collarbone. "I can heal them too. If it's not their time to die, I can heal supernatural things that are hurt back to health, so their glow disappears. But only if it's not their time. If it is, then I can't do anything but scream."

"That explains what happened with Joel."

"Yeah," I breathed.

He played with the ends of my hair. "Did you ask her about the aging? I know that it was something that you were interested to know."

I could feel my heart beating faster at the question and hoped that he didn't notice. His eyes narrowed. He had.

I tried to work it in my favour and forced a smile.

"Yes, and I will age." I nodded. "So we don't need to worry about you looking like an old man beside me."

"Well, that is a relief." Harper laughed.

I wrapped my arms around him, and he hugged me back, pressing his lips to my shoulder. I could feel his heart beating vigorously against mine and closed my eyes to remember the feeling, the sound – everything about that moment.

"Harper?"

"Mm?"

I bit my lip. "I really need to finish my homework."

He chuckled and loosened his hold on me, flinging himself back against my pillows again.

"No one is stopping you."

I groaned. "I am so going to fail."

Phase Six

The Death Wish

"Your brother is home," Harper said. He was still reclining on my bed, watching me scramble around my room as I gathered my things for uni. I tripped over a shoe.

"Was he out?"

"He's with a girl... Millie?" He frowned. His head was tipped as keys sounded in my front door.

I sighed. "Amelia Saber."

"The mayor's daughter?"

I picked up my leather jacket and pulled it on. It felt a bit snugger than it had before. I shrugged out of it and threw it at my desk.

"What's wrong?" he asked as he sat up. "Scorpion?"

"Not funny. It's too small."

Harper's arms folded over his knees. I threw his T-shirt at him, and he let it fall over his head.

"Taylor," he said. He picked it off and pulled it on.

"What?"

"You are enough."

I frowned. "I'm too much. I need to get healthy again."

"You are plenty healthy."

"I should run more."

He groaned and slid to the side of the bed, pulling on his jeans as he walked over towards me.

"You run through my mind all the time."

I elbowed him in the ribs, and he laughed as he moved his arms around me.

"You're not unhealthy," he murmured.

I pressed my face into his chest. "I suppose banshees don't need to worry about human health problems anyway. We have our own."

Harper pulled me back to look at me. "What do you mean?"

"What is this?" a male voice shouted. For a moment, I thought it was Jesse and he was aiming the question at me. But then I heard my brother's voice.

"What are you even doing here, Brandon?"

I stepped out of Harper's arms and went towards my door. I knew that this moment was inevitable as soon as I'd found out that Jesse was hooking up with Amelia. Even though she and Brandon were only together for a short time, he had really liked Amelia. Jesse would have known that. He should have told Brandon.

"Are you serious, bro? Is this who you've been going out with?" Brandon was still shouting.

I stepped into the doorway and felt Harper fall in behind me. Amelia looked over at us both, but the boys were too busy staring each other down.

Jesse exhaled. "Not that I need to *explain* myself to you—"

"Is this the other guy that you were talking about, Amelia? The one that you were interested in instead of me?" Brandon continued as he jabbed a finger at Jesse.

Amelia flushed scarlet. "I, well…"

"I thought that you were talking about that Marcus guy."

She blinked and then shuffled. "I should go."

"Good idea," Jesse replied as hurt flickered across Amelia's face.

"No," I called, breaking in between the tension. "Brandon can leave."

"It… it's fine, Taylor," she whispered. "I'll go."

Brandon's expression lifted. "Oh, you've met. Perfect, it's a family affair now."

"Brandon, just go." I groaned. "Go home."

"I'm going, it's fine," Amelia said.

I stared at Jesse, and he shrugged.

"You're not letting her leave like this, Jess," I hissed.

Jesse sat on a chair at the kitchen table. "If she wants to go, I'm not going to make her stay."

Amelia pressed her lips together, then slipped out the door. I wanted to scream at my brother for making her feel unwelcome when it was *Brandon* who was uninvited.

"How long has that been going on?" Brandon pressed. He was towering over Jesse now.

Jesse sighed. "B, you were with her for five minutes, quit acting like you were betrothed."

"I really liked her."

"Yet you didn't stay together. How is that my problem?"

Brandon frowned. "What is with you? The old Jesse wouldn't act like this – like he's never even *heard* of bro-code."

Jesse's grey eyes narrowed, and he stood up. He was taller than Brandon was when standing.

"The *old* Jesse?" he repeated. "You mean the Jesse who had a girlfriend who was *alive*?"

I glanced back at Harper who took a few steps forward, ready to break up the brawl that was threatened in Jesse's tone.

Brandon took a step back. "That... that's not... I didn't mean... Look, what happened to Ash—"

Jesse's fist clapped with Brandon's face before I had the chance to blink, and then Harper and I were lunging towards the two of them to pull them apart. Brandon wasn't putting up much of a fight, but my brother seemed to be using his best friend as some kind of aggression release.

Harper wrapped Jesse up while I pushed Brandon out of his reach.

Brandon wiped the blood off his mouth with his elbow. "I didn't even mean—"

"Just shut up, Brandon," I mumbled.

"I should be the one punching *him*."

I pushed him against the wall, and his eyes popped.

"Why?" I hissed. "Because she is offering my brother, your best friend, the support and comfort that neither of us can?"

He scoffed. "Support."

I pulled him forward, then pushed him back. "We were too close to him – to them as a couple. Jess needed someone who didn't know him with her, so back off and quit making this about you. This isn't about you."

161

Brandon frowned at me, then looked behind me. His eyes lowered to the floor.

"But why did it have to be Amelia?" he muttered.

I shoved him and stepped away. "Go ahead, Jess, he's all yours. A beating might do him good."

"I've already had one from the two of you. You're really strong, Taylor." Brandon sulked.

Harper smirked and released his restraint on Jesse. Jesse just sat back down at the table.

"Sorry," he breathed.

"Me too," Brandon mumbled. "Why didn't you just tell me about her?"

Jesse shrugged. "I knew that it would make you mad. I knew that you liked her."

I glanced at my watch. It was nearly ten o'clock. My lab workshop started in half an hour. I should make it, but depending on parking, I'd cut it close. I hadn't even had breakfast yet. I hated skipping meals, but I could see from here that the fruit bowl was empty. I was trying to think of whether I had an emergency muesli bar stashed in one of my bags.

"You're going to be late," Harper whispered. I looked up and found him in front of me.

"Yes."

"I'll drive you. It will save you finding a park."

I exhaled. Sometimes it bemused me how amazingly he could read me. "Thank you."

I dashed back to my room and grabbed my packed bag to meet Harper back in the place I'd left him.

"Now, can I leave without more blood being spilled?" I asked. "I have class."

Brandon and Jesse glanced up from their candid conversation.

"Have fun," Jesse said.

"Make them bleed, Tay." Brandon grinned.

Bygones. Boys were weird.

"One thirty, you finish?" Harper asked. He pulled my car up outside my building.

"Yes." I nodded. I opened the door and then groaned. "Ugh, I'm meeting Sal at one thirty though."

Harper's brow tightened. "Oh."

I shook my head. "I'm sorry. I don't have time... just come at one thirty. Meet me in the common room. I'm sure that he won't mind if you join us."

I didn't wait for a reply. I didn't want to give him the opportunity to say no or make any comments about *lunch-dates* that weren't dates.

I got to my lab ten minutes after it had started, and ended up having to work in the half-station in the corner of the room. My stomach growled for the second half of the three-hour workshop, but at least I had managed to scrimmage a dishevelled muesli bar in my uni bag. By the time class had finished, I had lost any ounce of care for a healthy diet. I felt like I was going to collapse.

Sal was sitting at the table right inside the door. I dropped my bag opposite him.

"You're late," he said.

"Sorry, I got held up."

He looked up from his watch. "Did your class just finish?"

"Lab, yes."

"You look tired."

"Thanks, I am," I groaned. "You hungry?"

"Starving. You?"

"Famished."

Sal frowned. "Unlike you. Missed lunch?"

"Breakfast."

"Really unlike you. How come?"

I rolled my eyes. "There was an incident at my apartment."

"Incident?"

"My brother tried to beat up his best friend after Brandon found out that Jesse was seeing his ex," I sighed.

Sal blinked. "Your brother, Jesse, beat up Brandon for finding out that Jesse was hooking up with *Brandon's* ex? Isn't that a bit backwards?"

"Maybe, but Brandon's a bit slow." I yawned. "I guess I owe you lunch, so what do you want? Half a cow? A platter of broiled bird? A pig on a spit?"

"I'm not Greek," he groaned.

I frowned. Greek. I wondered how Theo was doing.

"What's he doing here?" Sal asked.

My shoulders tensed, and I was almost too afraid to turn just in case it was Theo I'd see. Could he have recovered from a crushed windpipe in less than a week?

A warm hand smoothed over my neck, and I exhaled. Harper, it was Harper.

"*Bonjour, ma chérie.*" He smiled and leant to kiss me on the head. He placed a paper bag in front of me. I smirked at it.

"What's this?" I asked.

"Dinner, breakfast, lunch, whatever we're up to."

Sal scoffed, and I ignored him and opened the bag. Inside was a plastic container with salad and shreds of steak through it, and a little separate pot of dressing. Also in the bag was no-fat vanilla yoghurt and a tub of washed strawberries. I stared up at him incredulously.

"Where... what?" I sighed. "Thank you. I love you."

Sal stood up.

"Where are you going?" I asked.

"To get food," he mumbled. "I'm guessing wolf-wonder didn't pack anything in that little bag for me."

Harper sat down beside me on my left side, straddling the bench seat, so he was facing me. I reached in for the fork he'd packed. He hadn't forgotten anything. I was immensely impressed.

"How was the lab?" he asked.

"It was fine, but I got stuck at the worst station. You know the—"

"The corner one? That is the worst."

I smiled and shovelled the biggest spoonful I could jam on the fork into my mouth. I felt like I couldn't chew it fast enough for what my body was craving.

"So what else did you get up to?" I asked. "Apart from preparing me this banquet."

"I went to buy groceries to stock your fridge, and then went back to your place to check on Jesse," Harper explained. "Brandon had gone, so we spoke for a while as I organised this."

165

I had stopped chewing. "You spent time with my brother? Like, alone?"

He nodded. "I know that you're worried about him, and I heard what you said to Brandon. I didn't know Ashley very well, so I thought that I could offer him some company that won't make him feel her absence."

I dropped the fork and twisted to kiss him. He moved his hands around my middle.

"Ugh, gross. Are you trying to put me off my food?" Sal groaned.

I pressed one more kiss to Harper's lips, and then looked up at him.

"As if that's even possible," I replied.

Sal dropped his handful of food on the table that rivalled mine: a salad filled roll, a cookie, a tub of yoghurt, what smelt like pumpkin soup, a packet of pretzels, and an orange juice.

"Seriously," I sighed.

"Hey, you have three courses today."

"Two," I amended. "And I'm catching up on *breakfast*."

"Well, sue me, I'm hungry too." He shrugged. "I had breakfast early... at, like, nine."

"Nine o'clock is early?"

Sal sipped on the pumpkin soup. "Well, what time did you wake up?"

I glanced at Harper and pressed my lips together.

"Ugh, forget it, I don't want to know about your morning antics," Sal grumbled. "This third wheel stuff is excruciat—oh for the love of... don't eat my food, I'll be right back."

"Duty calls?" I asked.

Sal stood and grabbed the cookie. He sighed and headed down towards the toilets.

I nudged Harper. "Reaper duty."

"At least he gets a warning." Harper shrugged.

"True."

I continued eating my salad. I had finished it and began to pick at my strawberries before Sal finally returned. His usual chirpy demeanour was gone. He looked a little pale as he sat back down and dropped half of his cookie back on the table.

Harper shifted beside me. It was the first time I'd seen him with any kind of concern for the reaper. But anyone could see that something was wrong with Sal.

"Salvatore," I said.

It took a moment for his gaze to focus. He blinked up at me, and his orange eyes were swimming with intensity. I had only seen him after a couple of reaps, and it occurred to me that they weren't always quick and *easy*. Even if the one that I went on with him had taken it out of me, and affected my brother through our weird twin link.

I tried to smile at him, but he still looked like he had seen a ghost.

"Who was it?" Harper asked.

I had been trying to phrase the question but didn't know how to. I didn't know if I wanted to know, or if it would make a difference if he told me. I didn't know everyone in South Coast.

"Theo." Sal exhaled. His voice was barely audible, but I think that a part of me had expected to hear it. Theo was dead.

I was too afraid to ask if I had caused it because I knew that I had.

Harper's hand curled around mine.

"He remembered me," Sal murmured. He was looking at me as he spoke. "From the library. He made me work for it, for the reap."

"How?" I frowned. "How does someone make it harder for themselves to die?"

Sal looked at Harper, and their eyes clashed like their opposite colours on the colour wheel. I glanced between them, and the answer was on the tip of my tongue when Harper whispered it: "Suicide."

Sal nodded.

When reapers visited people before death, they took away their pain to relax their body so their soul could make the transition into their afterlife. If Theo had intended death, he could make it hurt on purpose, so when Sal took on his pain, it was transferred to him.

"Was he expecting you?" I asked.

His eyes traced back to me. "He was. It was like he wanted me to be there... like he did it to get me there."

"But he works on campus. He could have just found you here."

"What do you mean, *he wanted you there*? Like it was a lure?" Harper frowned. "Did he say anything?"

Sal shook his head. "No, he was choking up blood. But there was something written in... in his blood."

I shivered, and Harper's arm moved closer around me.

"What did it say?" he asked.

168

I felt sick, and Sal looked how I felt.

"It said…" he sighed. "It said, *she's next*."

"She?" Harper growled. "Taylor?"

Sal shrugged. "I… I can only assume. I… there was nothing else."

"But why would a wolf-hunter hunt a banshee?"

"I nearly killed him, that's why," I murmured. "He doesn't know what I am. He just knows that I'm not human."

"How did he do it?" Harper asked.

"A dagger," Sal breathed. "A silver dagger in his gut."

My hand lifted to my mouth. What a horrible way to die, even if he willed it.

Harper tipped his head. "Do you have a photo?"

Sal pulled a face. "What? No. Morbid much?"

"Why do you think that it was suicide?"

"There was no one else around." Sal shrugged. "And who else would target a wolf-hunter in that way?"

Harper exhaled and took out his phone. A few seconds later, he lifted it to his ear. Sal and I exchanged a look.

"Cole, it's Harper," he said into the handset. "The grim reaped the Greek a little while ago; suspected suicide; dagger. Do you know anyone at the coroner's office? Okay. Right, I didn't think of that. What about the autopsy? How long does that report take? You could? Great. There's something else. A message left in blood." Harper glanced at me. "*She's next*. We don't know. Perhaps. I don't either… you're right. That sounds fine. Thank you."

He lowered the phone, and I drew in a breath.

"What did he say?"

169

"Cole is going to get his hands on a copy of the medical notes when they come through. He's also looking into any potential police reports and the autopsy when it's prepared. That might be in a couple of days though."

"Doctor Vamp is connected, huh?" Sal mumbled.

Harper nodded. "If it was a threat from the Greek directed at Taylor, then we need to be prepared for what that could mean for all of us."

"You mean for you," Sal amended. "Because it would mean that more wolf-hunters are in town, and you'll be right beside Mistry on their most wanted list."

"Regardless, *Grim*, if Taylor's life is in danger, then I will make it my personal mission to keep her safe, whether that means my life is compromised or not."

"No," I said. "No, Harper, I don't want you involved if it means that you're in danger."

Harper sighed at me. "Taylor, please."

I knew it was useless, but I had to try. I knew that my days were numbered. I didn't like that the number seemed to be lower than I thought, but I knew the day was coming. I didn't fancy getting stabbed or anything though, even if a dagger seemed to be the only way that ensured my destruction.

I glanced down the common room and saw a black bird fly past the glass door at the far end. I stood up and saw the shadow creep into human form.

"Jenna," I breathed. I sat back down.

"Maybe she can help," Sal offered.

I looked at him, then back to the door as she opened it with a swoop and glided down the hall. Being winter term and

Friday afternoon, there were only a few other people in here. It was a relief really. In a typical term, we probably wouldn't have been able to speak so freely.

Jenna smiled as she came closer. Today she was sporting a black leather bodice with a black feathered skirt. She always seemed to have the appearance that she could take off and fly at any moment – and I guess she could. I noticed that today she didn't hide her scarred scratch. She wore it with pride, like a coat of arms.

"Taylor Mistry and her wolf pack." She smiled.

Sal huffed. "I'm not a dog."

"Were you looking for me?" I asked.

"Yes, Ruby thought that you may be here," she replied. "I flew by your unit, but there was no one home."

I nodded. "What do you need me for?"

"I wanted to settle a debt with you before I depart."

"You're leaving South Coast? Why?"

"It is soon time."

I bit my lip. "What debt?"

"You saved my life, Taylor," she said. "And for that, I offer you three wishes. But you know the drill, no love, no death, no life."

I blinked then shook my head. "I don't want any wishes, I don't need them."

Her eyebrows lifted over her black midnight eyes. "Excuse me?"

"I don't want anything to be handed to me." I shrugged. "If I've learnt anything in the past year, it's that the best things in life come because you work hard at them. It makes them worth it, it makes you appreciate them if you do things yourself rather than just acquire them."

"Well, I must say, I've never heard that one before," she said as she slipped in to sit beside Sal.

Harper looked at me with pride. "Taylor is unique."

"Different," Sal amended. "She's *different*."

Jenna took a deep breath. "Are you sure, Taylor? A wish from a djinn is not something to be refused lightly. We are the most powerful pure magic in existence."

"Harper said that you're a demi-god," I answered.

Jenna smiled at him.

"Cole said it first," he murmured.

"Hey, Mistry," Sal whispered. "Don't you want to wish the banshee away?"

I frowned in thought. "Becoming a banshee is what saved me. It was a consequence. If I weren't what I am, then it would probably only kill me sooner, right, Jenna?"

Jenna's head tipped. "It is not my place to offer advice for another's wish."

I nodded.

Sal strummed his fingers on the table. "Well, what about meeting Harper before the Italian wolf-hunter?"

I glanced at Harper. "But then I never would have met Ruby, or Cole, or even you, Sal. Everything that I am now is a result of what I've been through. It might not be carefree, but I feel like the people around me are what makes it bearable."

Jenna shook her head incredulously. "A very peculiar girl. You are actually grateful for your shortcomings."

"Overcoming weaknesses is what makes you strong," I replied. As I spoke, I thought of my efforts in losing weight and the struggle it had been to maintain. I remembered reaching a point where I realised that it didn't matter what I weighed, it only mattered what attitude I had towards myself because that was what people saw and responded to. It seemed almost ironic to me that something so first world like gaining weight would alter that attitude, even if I knew that it was nonsense. Maybe I was vain. Maybe I was ridiculous and selfish to think that the way I looked mattered to others, but what was important was that it mattered to me. So I had to admit that, at that moment, I took pause and wondered if I could just wish it all away. The constant struggle, the exertion I put into just feeling normal, and the disappointment that came with falling short of my own expectations. Would it change me to wish for control over something that I had always battled? Was it worth the risk?

Jenna and Harper watched me as I wrestled with my internal demons. Sal seemed to be finally getting his appetite back and was picking at the array of food still in front of him.

Harper's hand squeezed my knee, and I looked over at him. He gave me a reassuring smile that made me think that he was proud that I didn't wish for anything more in my life. I wondered what he would think if he knew that I wanted something so superficial.

"Well, Taylor Mistry," Jenna said, and I wondered if she could read the indecision in my eyes. "As I am still interested in speaking more with Cole about his experiences, I will give you until the next Full Moon to think about my offer and give me your final answer."

"I… okay." I nodded. "So you'll stay until then?"

The next Full Moon was two weeks and two days away. I was a little relieved that she had given me so much time to think about anything I wanted. I wished that I had the strength and determination to confidently refuse them now, but I couldn't deny that as I thought about the possibilities for the wishes, and the temptation was seizing me.

"Yes, until the next Full Moon," she replied.

"Hey, Djinn Jenna?" Sal said.

I rolled my eyes.

Jenna sighed. "Yes, Reaper Salvatore?"

"You can't make people fall in love, or kill people, or bring them back to life, but what about changing their fate?" he asked.

"Fate? No. A person's fate is tied to who or what they love. Only they have the power to change it if they so choose," she answered. "Why do you ask?"

Sal glanced at me, and Jenna followed his eyes.

"Do you seek to change your fate, Taylor?"

I shook my head. "Not when it comes to love. Though, I fear that my fate has nothing to do with love. I think it has more to do with revenge."

"No one will get close, I won't allow it," Harper said.

"Did something happen?" Jenna asked. "Are you in danger?"

"Well—" I started.

"Yes," Sal replied.

"Perhaps," Harper amended.

Jenna shook her head, and her glossy black hair swirled over her shoulders.

"Start from the beginning, Taylor."

Sal took a breath. "Once upon a time—"

"I said *Taylor*," Jenna said evenly. "Go on, Taylor."

Salvatore Vincent, making friends wherever he goes.

I exhaled. "Well, it all started. When did it start? After the last Full Moon, a few weeks ago. Theo saw Harper in the admin building when I was getting a new student ID because I stupidly lost the last one—"

"Taylor, relevance," Sal groaned.

"Who is Theo?" Jenna asked.

I shook my head. "Sorry, Theo is a wolf-hunter… *was* a wolf-hunter."

"I see."

"And he recognised Harper; he knew what he was, so we were careful that he wouldn't see us—"

"Taylorrrrrr," Sal groaned. "Need to know basis."

I threw a strawberry at him, and it bounced off his cheek. He frowned at it, and then ate it off the table. I rolled my eyes.

"Theo came after me in the library," I continued. "He suspected that I was something; he threw colloidal silver on me and stabbed me with a knife. A regular knife."

Jenna's brows were drawn. "I see."

"So I, in an entirely self-preservation move, crushed his windpipe."

"I see." She smirked.

"Sal stopped me from killing him, but just now he died. We think that it might have been suicide, but written beside him in his blood was a message. *She's next.*"

"She?" Jenna repeated. "You?"

I shrugged. "I don't know. We don't know for sure, but I don't know who else it would be. Theo knew that Sal existed because he knows about the supernatural world. We think that maybe he intended Sal to go and see it. Maybe he's alerted other wolf-hunters, and he's messing with us."

"I see." She nodded.

Sal threw his hands up in the air. "She's not exactly painting a canvas there, Djinn, what do you see?"

Jenna glared at Sal. "It's all highly suspicious."

"Well, gold star to you." He huffed. "Tell us something we don't know."

"Why would he give you a warning if that's what he has done?" she asked. "I have no need to strategise, but I would think that in an attack, the element of surprise is more advantageous than warning your enemy that you're coming."

Harper nodded. "That's what I think."

"Or maybe he's just trying to make us suffer slowly and be paranoid until his Greek relatives roll into town." Sal offered.

"Well, in regards to this kind of fate, Taylor Mistry, I'm afraid that not even you can help that," she said. "For other kinds of supernatural beings, they can choose when their time is up, or have it stolen away from them through being killed, but banshees are not the same."

Harper sat forward. "What do you mean?"

"Taylor has a time limit, she is at her own crossroads between the supernatural and human, life and death," Jenna explained. "Banshees, therefore, adhere to all rules when it comes to living and dying, both in the supernatural and the natural world. They are strong and impenetrable unless pierced with silver. Though they can heal, they can still be harmed or killed with a spelled dagger to the heart. They will age and, for that reason, like humans, or their human-reaper counterpart, their time will run out just the same. They do not experience death in the same way as everyone else, for they have already experienced it. Taylor was correct before in saying before that wishing away the banshee in her would result in her human death. The supernatural element in her is what is keeping her alive. Her human body died when she was transformed into the white woman, much in the way that Salvatore traded his death for a life as a reaper."

Sal was frowning deeply. "I thought it wasn't your place to offer advice for another's wish."

Jenna lifted an eyebrow. "That was not advice, that was fact… and Taylor was not making a wish."

Harper was a statue beside me. I could feel the tension rolling from him as if he was an elastic band that was stretched to its limit. Jenna had just told him that from the moment I was marked, my death was inevitable, and it was something that, in one way, I had already experienced and would experience again. To him, I knew that he would think that he had failed in his attempt to save my life after I'd saved his. I saw a flash around him from the corner of my eye and looked over at him. His eyes were swimming with every emotion that I hated to see in them: guilt, sorrow, pity, anger, hopelessness, desperation...

"Don't," I breathed as my fingers brushed his cheeks. "I'm okay. I'm here. I'm alive."

I lifted his hand to my chest. My heart was beating fast from stress, but I was glad for it. It made it sound vital, and it was.

Harper's head shook.

"I don't regret anything, I would do it again," I whispered. "Don't you go thinking that any of this was your fault. I would stop that car every time to save you, Harper. Every time."

His head turned, and my hand moved to catch moisture that trickled from it. I climbed up onto his lap and hugged him. At first, his arms were rigid, and then they were crushing me against him.

I couldn't hear any noise from Sal or Jenna. I didn't know if they were making any. I just knew that everything that had been said had changed everyone's outlook on everything. I coupled it with the notion that I was not expected to live until I was old and grey as a banshee; along with the realisation that each day was even more precious. It was overwhelming. Taylor Mistry, human Taylor Mistry was no longer. The essence of who I was only lived on because of a supernatural force, a presence, much like the vampires. I may be much more durable than my immortal counterpart, but it was for a much shorter time.

It was minutes before I felt strong enough to loosen my grip on Harper, and I wasn't sure whether it was because I was scared that he would fall apart or I would. I brushed his face and slid back beside him. I pressed his hands to my lips.

"I'm sorry," Jenna sighed. "I didn't mean to upset you both."

I sniffled. "You didn't do anything but tell us the truth. We're better off knowing so that we can be prepared for what may come."

Harper didn't speak, but he squeezed my hand. I squeezed it back.

"We've overcome obstacles before," I said. "We've beaten the odds when the odds were against us, so I don't care about the rest of it. I believe that we can make it through. I won't give up on us."

He nodded.

"So what happens now?" Sal asked. "What do we do about Theo?"

"Nothing," I answered. "Cole is going to get back to us about his death. Until then, I am going to focus on what I can control, not what I can't."

Sal looked at me as if I'd gone crazy. "Nothing?"

I nodded. "I'm going home. It's Friday, my classes are finished, and I want to spend some quality time with my boyfriend."

Sal pulled a face.

Jenna smiled weakly, but her eyes looked wary.

I stood up and pulled Harper with me, gathered my packed lunch with my free hand, and shoved it in my uni bag.

"Thank you for lunch, Sal," I said. "Jenna, thank you for coming. We'll see you two soon."

I turned and tugged Harper along with me. As soon as we reached outside, he seemed to thaw, but he still didn't speak until we were inside my car. I considered offering to drive, but the way he was looking at me was as if he was about to raid a cotton factory and wrap me up in it.

"I don't want you to pity me," I murmured. "I don't want you to treat me as if I'm going to break. I'm not broken, I'm just different. I'm still me though."

"I know, and I love you. I just—"

"Nope," I said. "Don't. Love is enough."

He reached for my hand, and I took his. He didn't let go until we were back at my unit and we needed to let go to exit the car.

He didn't leave my side, and I didn't want him to. We stayed linked, never apart, and remained that way through the night and into the next day.

I didn't need to be anywhere, so I didn't go. We only left my room for food and, even then, it wasn't for long. We didn't say much because words were not enough. Words couldn't describe how it felt to know that sometimes love wasn't enough. Love could do a lot of things, but it couldn't conquer death, but it could outlast it.

"We've been in bed, like, all day. We might have to leave my unit tomorrow. Even for a little while," I murmured. The sun had been and gone on Saturday, it was nearing eleven o'clock. There was only the glow of my lamp to light my room.

Harper's eyes were closed, but he smiled. "Fine, we can leave to go to my apartment and stay there."

I laughed. "Okay, deal. Besides, Cole might have some news by then."

Harper's eyes opened. "Yes. Perhaps."

"Knowledge is power," I whispered. My fingers traced his lips. "The more we know, the more prepared we'll be."

"True," he breathed.

His lips turned down, and I leant forward and pressed mine to them. He pulled me against him, and I melted into him. When it came time, and breathing became more of a necessity, we parted, and I rested my head on his chest. Harper's fingers ran up and down my back as I thought over what Jenna had told me about banshees. It was a lot of information in a short space of time, considering I had been the creature in full form for only two weeks. I thought about what I could offer for the other supernatural beings out there, and my mind wandered back to the last Full Moon, my first Full Moon, when André and Hunter had fought against me for their life. It made no sense for them to resist me so much if it was true that their will that brought me there. I shouldn't have even been there unless they had some kind of death wish. So why was I there? Did the two of them have a reason to die, like Jenna had said? There was no possible way to ask André, and even though Hunter was back in town, she'd sooner stab me again than shed any light on the question.

It occurred to me, as I listened to the steady *thud* of Harper's heart that the two of them weren't alone that night. The answer might be right under my nose.

I straightened my head and rested my chin on Harper's chest.

181

"Harper?"

"Mm?"

"You were there the night of the Full Moon with Hunter and André. Do you remember hearing either of them saying anything about dying or wanting to die?" I asked. It was a long shot, but I had to try.

Harper frowned in thought. "I was in transformation, so I... I can't be sure. Why? Is it important?"

"A little." I shrugged. "Banshees don't hunt; they just follow the glow of those who wish to crossover, or those dying. Since neither of them appeared to be hurt before I got there, there must have been a reason why I was drawn to them. I just wanted to know if you knew what it was."

"I cannot..." Harper sighed and gnawed on his lower lip. "The only thing I can think of is that I remember André saying something to the effect that he would die to protect Hunter. She was telling him about her brush with the wendigo. I think that it was shortly before the Moon's apex."

I frowned. "Well, that's something, I guess, but I don't think that explains why he *wanted* to die that night. Hunter's glow was so bright in itself and, yet, she was fighting me... they both were. Neither of them seemed like they *wanted* to die."

Harper wrapped his arms around me. "Do not worry yourself trying to understand Hunter. She is temperamental and volatile, and to be quite honest, I never really could understand her thought process."

"But she was always loyal to you," I said. "She must have really loved you to still help to save me when she hated me from the outset."

He looked down at me then tucked my hair behind my ear. "She only hated you because she knew that I loved you. When I first told her about you, about how you'd saved me, she urged me to leave, but I couldn't. I needed to know you."

"She was jealous." I nodded. "Understandable."

"It didn't matter to me what she was, what mattered was your safety."

I pressed my lips together.

"What is it?" he asked. "What's wrong?"

I shook my head. "Nothing. I just, well I suppose I never really had the opportunity to warm to Hunter because she resented me for who I was to you. But I kind of feel sorry for her."

"Why?"

"Because you... you were together for a while, and it's evident that she cares so much for you."

"Taylor, she and I—"

"I know that you were friends, and you are just friends now, but I can understand that she would feel, well, a little scorned by the fact that you moved on and she had to see you with someone else. If that were me—"

"Taylor," he sighed. "There will never be anyone else but you."

I nodded. "All I'm saying is that I feel sorry for her. I took you away from her and then reaped her friend. I understand why she came after me the way she did."

"You didn't take me away from her, we remained friends after you and I got together."

"That's not the same, and you know it," I answered.

He smiled weakly. "Perhaps."

I yawned.

"Time for sleep," he whispered. He touched his index finger to my nose. I rolled over, and he moved in behind me, wrapping me in his warm arms. I would probably need to invest in an air-conditioner for my room for the summer because the heat from him would be too much, and yet, I couldn't imagine not having him here with me. If I was still around by then.

"Harper, can you reach the lamp without moving?" I breathed. "I'm too comfortable to move."

He breathed a laugh. "It is out, Taylor."

My eyes shot open, and I sat up with a start. "Oh, n… oh. Oh no."

"What?" He frowned.

"The light," I sighed. "It's coming from me."

Phase Seven

The Hunted

"What does it mean, Cole?" Harper demanded. He was making the two of us nervous as he paced up and down Cole's study. Ruby was still at Crescent since Saturdays were their busiest nights. It was about midnight now, and we had been at Cole's apartments for about half an hour. Needless to say, it wasn't the first time that Harper had asked Cole that question.

"Harper, I—" Cole started.

"How do we make it stop?" Harper asked. It wasn't the first time he'd asked that either.

Cole glanced at me, and I stood up from one of the couches.

"Harper, please sit down," I said. "You're wearing a hole in the carpet."

"This is your life that we're talking about, I'm not sitting down until I know that you are out of harm's way," he answered. It felt like an odd kind of déjà vu, except that this time, we had no idea what was hunting me – if it was even a *something*. It could be something as simple and unbeatable as the time that I was up against.

"Then you could be standing for a long time," I sighed.

Harper stopped pacing and shook his head at me. "This is not funny."

"No one is laughing," I replied. "I just... getting mad at Cole isn't going to fix it, nor is vowing to stand. So just sit down and let's just try to come up with something practical."

Harper exhaled and folded into the couch. He dropped his head into his hands.

"I am sorry. I'm sorry, Cole, I'm just..."

"You don't need to explain, friend," Cole said with a nod. "I would be the same if it were Ruby we were talking about, worse even."

Harper looked up. "So what do we do? When... what do we do?"

Cole glanced at me. "How bright is it, Taylor?"

I lifted my hand. "I can show you if you have a dimmer switch somewhere in the apartment."

Cole smiled. "You could, but I'm afraid that the intensity means more to you than it would to me. Perhaps if you compare it to the illumination of André's glow."

"It's not as bright as that, it's somewhere between that and you," I replied. "But it's a constant glow, a definite radiance."

Cole nodded. "Well, at least you're not at the brightness of that status."

Death status.

"Do you think that another banshee will come for me if I do?" I asked. "That is, if I reach André's level."

Harper made a low growling-whimpering sound.

Cole shook his head. "I, uh..."

"No, they wouldn't. Jenna said that I had already technically died, and Sal wasn't at that reaping since I became this instead," I answered. "I suppose whatever happens to vampires when they die will happen to me. Banshees are like the anti-vampires."

Cole brushed his blond hair out of his eyes. "Could we speak to Jenna? Perhaps she could—"

"No, she can't bestow love, death, or life on people," I sighed. "This one is on me."

Cole nodded and then looked down as he pulled his phone out from his pocket. Harper looked up, but I couldn't hear a thing. It must have been on vibrate. Vampires didn't need it on loud since their hearing was better than a wolf's.

"Excuse me, it's the hospital," Cole murmured.

Harper turned fully towards him as the vampire answered the call. I felt like a poor excuse for a supernatural creature. Banshees didn't get high definition hearing.

I watched Cole's expression for a while and then turned my attention to Harper. Cole was well trained at keeping an even façade, but Harper was as readable as a billboard. His peaked interest morphed into curiosity, and like the sun setting, his olive-green eyes dimmed into a deep avocado-colour.

"What is it?" I whispered.

Harper lifted his finger. A moment later, Cole lowered his phone.

"Well?" I prompted. "Was that about Theo's autopsy?"

Cole nodded. "The wound doesn't appear to be self-inflicted. The angle of the knife was wrong for suicide."

I exhaled. "Good news or bad news?"

"What was that about the tooth?" Harper frowned. "I missed it."

"Tooth?"

Cole rubbed his jaw, and I took a moment to marvel at how amazing he was at playing a human.

"He was missing one of his canines," Cole replied. "It had been forcibly removed."

I blinked. "What? Who would do that?"

"I don't know, I'm sorry," Cole sighed. "It is all rather perplexing, but at least we know that whoever murdered Theo did so for a reason. That message was intended for someone, and I agree that Sal is a possible target for it. The next thing that we need to figure out is who *she* is, and—"

"And if it's Taylor?" Harper asked.

"*If* it is then we can narrow down suspects for people who have a problem with Taylor, but who have no trepidation in killing a wolf-hunter."

I sighed. "Simple as that."

"So, where do we start?" Harper murmured.

I yawned, and Cole glanced at me.

"Sleep," he said. "There's nothing that we can really do right now, unfortunately."

Harper stood. "Cole, we need to—"

"Harper, I understand, really," Cole interrupted. He rested a hand on Harper's shoulder. "But it's the middle of the night, and losing sleep will not benefit Taylor. We can reassess our options in the morning, and I'll do some digging until then. We won't let anything happen to her. You have my word."

Harper stared at Cole for a few moments, and then eventually nodded. I was pleased that at least Cole had calmed him a little. I wasn't thrilled about having a glow and being able to see that my life now had a time limit, like some kind of weird sands through an hourglass, or a kettle that was coming to the boil. Plus, the prospect of a new threat seemed a little excessive even for us. I appreciated that Cole had made it sound like we could do something to change my fate, but I feared that it was just as Jenna had said on Friday afternoon – that we all choose our destiny depending on those that we love.

I still wouldn't have chosen any differently.

We stayed in Harper's apartment to sleep because it was only down a few floors from the vampires. Harper also didn't want to tempt fate by driving home on a Saturday after midnight. South Coast was usually a quiet little city, but it had its moments. I knew firsthand about those other moments, so I didn't argue with him. Besides, I was getting sick of the sight of my room.

I couldn't sleep. I couldn't close my eyes, because I felt like I was missing out on something that I wouldn't get to experience again. Or maybe that I was just wasting what time I had left. It was amazing what happened when you realised that your days, your hours, your minutes, your seconds, were numbered. I think that there are times when everyone considers their mortality. Maybe they write a *bucket list* or take a chance that they otherwise wouldn't take. Everyone takes into account that one day they will cease to exist—they might not entirely be able to comprehend it since we all picture the future with ourselves in it—but we all ponder the prospect at some point.

Harper wasn't coping with even the contemplation of my impending demise, much the same way that I couldn't bring myself to ever consider the thought of my world without him. Regardless, I knew that it was something that we needed to think about.

"No, Taylor," Harper sighed. "I will not humour the thought because I will not allow it. If that is your fate, then we will change it. Together we will change it."

"Okay, sure, we can try. But, Harper—"

"No. No buts."

My eyes closed. "I need to know that you won't give up. I need to know that you'll be okay if—"

"No. I am not... we are not having this conversation. I'm not giving up, not now, not ever. Not without you."

"Harper," I breathed.

"Taylor, look at me," he said. His hands rested on my face. "Don't give up. We'll fight this. You said so yourself that we have overcome worse."

I nodded.

"Such is life," he sighed. "Such is fate."

I tried to smile, and he seemed satisfied with what I came up with. Harper wrapped his arms around me. I was tired of feeling sad.

"I need to change my clothes," I mumbled against his arm. "I'm still in my pyjamas, and I can't spend another day in the same clothes."

He laughed quietly and kissed my head. "Okay, let me get my helmet."

I frowned. "But my car is in the garage."

"I know, but I'm not tempting fate even in the slightest."

I rolled my eyes.

On the drive home, I considered lying to him, to all of them. I thought about just telling them that the glow had dimmed, and my life was no longer in peril, or whatever was happening. I thought about it, but I couldn't bring myself to tell it.

Maybe I was selfish. Maybe I wanted them to fuss over me. To try to save me as they had once before and succeeded... sort of. Maybe I just didn't want to give up.

"There's a box on your doorstep," Harper murmured. He took a deep breath. "I can smell something sweet, but I don't know..."

"Can you hear it ticking?" I asked.

He blinked at me. "No."

"Great," I sighed. I took a step forward, but Harper stopped me. "Harper, its Sunday. Whatever it is, it's probably something from Brandon, or my parents, or something."

"Possibly," he said.

I pressed my lips together and waited. A decent few seconds had passed before he lowered his arm, but caught my hand in his. He guided me forward slowly.

"It's definitely sweet," he said. "Sugary sweet."

"Weird. It's probably for Jesse."

Harper glanced at me, and then stopped in front of the white foam box. It was about the size of an A3 piece of paper. He lowered to kneel and then let go of my hand to open the lid. I bobbed around his arms to see what was inside.

"Doughnuts," Harper murmured. "With your name all over them."

"What?" I asked.

I peered in the box filled to the brim with assorted colours and flavours of the sugary pastry; every single one of them bearing *Taylor* in perfect icing script. I glanced at Harper and then looked around.

"Who would have done that?" I frowned. "Is this some kind of terrible joke?"

He put the lid back on the box to cover the sickly sweet smell.

"It's something."

"Is there anything else that you can smell? Did whoever left them leave a scent or… or something?"

His head shook. "All I smell is sugar and cat."

I exhaled and straightened to unlock the door. "I need to feed Raven."

"I'll dispose of these," he said. He picked up the box and allowed me to open the screen door. "We do not know who left them."

I unlocked the wooden door and pushed it open. "Do you really think someone is going to poison me with doughnuts?"

"I don't like to think that anyone would *want* to hurt you, Taylor, but I won't take any chances."

"Fine then, throw them out." I shrugged. "I just hate to waste food."

Harper and I both looked up as the scraping of feet sounded down the driveway. Then the blond tuft of Brandon's hair appeared.

"Oh, hi," he said. "What's in the box?"

"Rubbish," I replied.

Harper twisted away from him, but Brandon lifted the lid. I wasn't really surprised considering he was always interfering and inviting himself into other people's business.

"They're Taylor doughnuts." He frowned. "Why are there so many? How come you're throwing them out? Where did they come from? Who—?"

"Brandon, shut up." I groaned. "I don't know, to all of the above."

He pouted at them, and then picked one up. In the same second, he had bitten into it.

"No—" Harper and I shouted. Our voices seemed to harmonise.

"What?" Brandon gulped. "Is there something wrong with them?"

Harper tipped his head. "I guess we're going to find out."

"Huh?"

"Brandon, come inside," I sighed. I scratched my head. "Harper just… just bring the doughnuts in. We might need the rest of them if there is something wrong with them."

"I'm totally confused," Brandon mumbled. "Do you expect there to be something wrong with them? They taste fine to me. Why were you just going to throw them out? Why are you still in your pyjamas, Taylor?"

I took a deep breath. "I'm going to get a shower. Harper, keep an eye on him."

"You're kidding right?" Brandon laughed and looked to Harper. "She's kidding, isn't she?"

"About the shower? Probably not." Harper shrugged.

I laughed. I didn't mean to, considering that Brandon could keel over at any moment. But it was unlike Harper to make any attempt at humour.

Brandon's eyebrows drew. He coughed.

"You okay?" I asked.

"Other than the fact that I'm a little scared you're showing any kind of concern for me, Tay, I'm peachy," he answered. "But seriously, can I eat all of these? They're amazing."

I glanced at Harper, then looked back to Brandon.

"Maybe just pace yourself."

"Why do they have your name on them? Were they a present?" he asked.

I shrugged. "We're still trying to figure that one out."

"Pretty good present. I mean, maybe not for you since you're all healthy and stuff, and freak out at the sight of dessert but—"

"You're right." I frowned. "I do freak out at the sight of dessert. Everyone who knows me knows that. Maybe the only thing wrong with them is that they're sugary."

Harper folded his arms. "You think that whoever sent them was just trying to tempt you?"

"It seems so petty," I sighed.

"And expensive. These are quality." Brandon nodded. I noticed that he was on his second doughnut, and I resented him a little for having the metabolism of an athlete. Not enough to wish death upon him though.

"What did I say about pacing yourself?" I snapped.

He shrugged. "Weren't you getting a shower? I guess you were kidding about that."

I shook my head and turned towards my room.

Well, at least I tried.

*

Brandon didn't die. But he did complain about having a sore stomach after eating three of the sugary pastries within the space of ten minutes of setting eyes on them. My sympathy was in short supply.

Harper kept a watchful eye on me as I kicked things around the floor of my room to clean it, and then rifled through my uni bag to find all the readings and exercises that I needed to do in preparation for my last week of class.

The illumination was distracting, but I was getting better at ignoring it. It was a constant glow, after all, and eventually, I became resided to the fact that my naturally tanned-looking skin appeared more vampire-pale now that I was in the twilight hours of my life. What I found that was the strangest thing though, was that my reflection still looked like me... the me that everyone else saw. I guess it was poetic considering I had always seen myself differently to the way that everyone else saw me.

"Harper, have you seen my necklace?" I asked. It was Monday morning, and I had just finished brushing my teeth after breakfast.

He appeared in the doorway. "Your necklace?"

"The one that you gave me. Your wolf tooth." I frowned. "I swear that I had it on yesterday, but today it's gone."

"Perhaps the cord broke?"

I checked my watch. "I'm going to be late if I don't leave now. I'll have to look for it after uni. Or you could look while I'm gone?"

"I'm coming with you, Taylor," he replied. He said it as if I had merely forgotten that he was in my class. But he wasn't. This was something else.

"Harper, you don't need to—"

"Please," he sighed. "There is no point in arguing."

I exhaled. "Fine. Let's go."

There was a part of me that questioned my own sanity about continuing with winter term despite the fact I may not be around to finish my degree. Harper understood though, he held education at the same high regard that I did. It was ingrained in me from a young age that knowledge was power. Learning and studying had been the only thing for a long time that I could control in my life, and in a way, it still was. Plus, the fact that I deemed it appropriate to continue my studies demonstrated to Harper that I still hadn't given up on finding a way to change my fate.

When class finished, I found Harper outside the door sitting with Sal. I had a feeling that my days would consist of this from now until I either glowed bright or didn't glow at all.

"Greetings, Taylor Maye Mistry." Sal grinned. "What did you learn today?"

"That apparently everyone in my life is as paranoid as Harper."

Sal sat back. "You look different."

"You're not funny."

"I'm not trying to be. I can see your energy. I couldn't before."

I folded my arms. "What does that mean?"

"I don't know. It's very faint, feathery," he mused. "Comes and goes like a flicker of darkness."

"Darkness means death to reapers," Harper said. He was beside me in an instant as if his closeness could cure me.

"Only for humans, Taylor isn't human," Sal replied. "Well, I guess a part of her must still be."

"Well, I'm not part cyborg, despite the silver in my veins," I sighed. "Come on, Harper. I want to find my necklace."

"Taylor," Sal said. His hand caught my wrist. "Harper told me that you can see your light. I want to help."

"How?"

He shrugged. "However I can."

I nodded. "Thanks, but I'm not even sure how we can help what's coming."

Sal glanced at Harper. "Giving up mentally is part of it, Mistry. Don't think negative. Your mind has more power than you realise."

I rolled my eyes. "What are you even talking about?"

"Joel," Harper murmured. "You might have healed him with your physical presence, but you spoke to him too. You healed his thoughts, his mind."

"That makes no logical sense."

"Does any of it?" Sal countered. "What is logical about what you are?"

"You healed me too, Taylor," Harper said. "You saving me gave me a reason to live. I could feel it when you saw my light. I could feel the change in myself because it stemmed from my thoughts that there was no hope. You gave me hope then too."

My head shook. "Harper, I really think you've been spending too much time with Sal."

"Life is more philosophical than you care to admit, Taylor Mistry," Sal replied. "Science can only explain the explainable. We all live in a world that falls short of science. You need to believe in it, or you might as well just give up now. Knowledge is powerful, but so is wishful thinking."

I looked up at Harper who ran his fingers down my cheek. I had told him once before that wishful thinking was what had made me sure that he would come back to me after the wendigo and banshee attack. At the time, I was trying to make a point that I hadn't given up on him. I realised now, as I stared into his olive-green eyes, that he was only asking me to have that same faith again.

"Such is fate," I whispered.

Harper's face softened into a small smile of relief. He pressed his lips to my forehead.

Sal just sighed. "I really think you missed the entire point of my little speech there, Mistry."

"I heard you, Sal." I nodded. "Mind over matter."

"Blasphemy," he gasped. "And here I thought that you were a scientist."

*

On Tuesday, Harper and Sal continued their strange truce as they tagged-teamed their surveillance over me. Sal even convinced my tutor into letting him audit the class. By the time lunchtime came, I was relieved for at least the distraction of food amongst us to break the tension.

"Still haven't found your necklace?" Sal asked. "Have you checked your car?"

I spread my hand over my collarbone. "Yes, I've looked. And no, I haven't found it yet."

"Well, no one would have stolen it. It's not exactly the crown jewel."

"It was to me." I frowned.

Harper took a sip of my diet coke and put it back in front of me. I took another bite of my wrap.

"Hey, Djinn, to what do we owe the pleasure?" Sal said over the top of me.

"Reaper." Jenna nodded. "Again, I was looking for Taylor."

"What's up, Jenna?" I asked. "I thought I had another week or so to give you my ans—"

"It's not about the wishes." She smiled. "It's about something else."

Jenna fluttered around to sit beside Sal. Today she wore a cotton maxi-dress with material that was patterned in a design that resembled feathers. Her dark hair was up and fastened with a hair stick that had two black feathers hanging from it.

"Cole informed you of our predicament?" Harper said. It almost wasn't a question, but Jenna treated it as much.

She nodded. "I want to help."

"How?" Sal asked. "Can you magic the glow away? Can you extend her life?"

"No, as I said I can't use my powers to manipulate death or life—"

"Well, have you at least seen this kind of thing before?"

"Not in someone as young as Taylor," she answered. "Normally it's towards the end of the banshee's lifespan."

Sal shifted. "And what age is that?"

Jenna glanced at me. "Thirty-five… give or take a few years."

Harper's eyes closed and I watched as the glow around him began to brighten.

"That probably wasn't helpful, Jenna," I mumbled. "I can see Harper's glow now."

Sal threw one of his grapes at Harper, and Harper's eyes opened.

"Snap out of it, Wolfie, Taylor has enough to worry about without you giving up too," Sal said.

Harper nodded and drew in a breath. In front of my eyes, I saw the glow fade. It was remarkable.

"How did you do that?" I frowned. "You made it go away."

Harper looked at me, curling his hand around mine. "I reminded myself of everything that I have to live for."

"Well, I don't want to die," I sighed. "Do you think that it's as easy as me deciding to live?"

"I don't know," he answered. "I don't know what to do or how to make it better. I don't know how to protect you, because I don't know what the threat is. I don't know what is causing it, or who is causing it. I just don't know, Taylor. That thought, alone, is killing me because all I've ever wanted to do from the second I set eyes on you is protect you. I can't even consider that if… when we get past this obstacle, that you could only have another ten or twelve years left of your life. I just can't."

I shuffled against his side and rested my head on his shoulder. "Okay. I'm sorry. I know. I'm sorry."

Sal and Jenna exchanged a look. It was almost awkward, like they were intruding on our moment, but also mixed with a kind of resignation and determination.

"One thing at a time." Sal frowned.

Jenna leant forward and ran her hand over the scratch-scar on her forearm.

"Taylor, tell me, what were you doing when you noticed the, uh, change?" she asked. "Something must have set it off."

I swallowed. "You don't think that it's just my time to die?"

"You're twenty-two, you've been a full banshee for less than a month," she replied. "Not in the slightest."

I drew in a breath. "I don't know. I noticed it when we were trying to get to sleep. I thought the lamp was still on in my room."

Jenna glanced at Harper. "Anything else that you can remember? Were you talking or…?"

"Spare us the play-by-play," Sal added.

I glared at him. "We weren't *doing* anything but trying to sleep."

201

"We were talking." Harper frowned. "You were asking me about André and Hunter. You wanted to know if they wanted to die last Full Moon."

"That's right." I nodded.

"I remember you mentioning them since you thought that they were fighting you to stay alive," Jenna replied. "André was the one that you reaped, but who is Hunter again?"

"Hunter is the were-panther that gave you that scratch," I answered. I nodded towards the scar under her fingers. It was a few shades lighter than the rest of her lovely brown skin.

Jenna's eyes seemed to blaze with fire. "I see."

"Hunter did that?" Harper frowned.

"The black jaguar, yes," Jenna murmured. "Taylor, did you find out why you were beaconed to reap the two of them?"

I shook my head. "Harper thought he heard André say something about him being willing to die for Hunter, but that doesn't mean that he—"

"He would die for her?" Jenna frowned. "She is a shifter; she is not in danger of dying unless something was hunting her."

"Well, at the time, I think she thought I was."

"But you weren't, because you don't," Jenna answered. "Is there another reason why this Hunter-panther would want to die?"

I glanced at Harper and then pressed my lips together.

"What?" Harper shrugged. "I did not want her to die."

"But she would have died for you," I replied. "When she agreed to help save me, it was only in concern for your *suicide mission*. Remember?"

Harper shook his head. "But she stabbed me, Taylor."

I sighed. "Yes, but she was aiming for me. You should have seen her face when you knocked her away from me. She looked so shocked. It was almost as if she expected you to attack me instead."

Jenna glanced at Sal and lifted her eyebrows.

"I get the feeling that the panther did not like you, Taylor," Jenna said.

"No, she didn't," I said. "Even when she was trying to protect me, it was all for Harper. She told me once not to bother falling for him because whatever he felt for me wouldn't last."

"What?" Harper frowned. "You never told me that."

"It wasn't worth mentioning."

"She was quite jealous of you then," Jenna mused.

"I guess a little." I shrugged. "She and Harper were... close before I came along."

All eyes turned on Harper, and he rolled his light green eyes.

"We were never serious," he mumbled.

I shook my head. "Anyway, of course, after Harper and I got together, the Full Moon happened, and I took her friend André from her. I haven't seen her since, which is probably a good thing for both of us. If she didn't hate me before, I'm sure she does now."

Jenna leant on her elbow and frowned.

"What are you thinking, Djinn?" Sal asked.

"I am thinking... of the lengths that some may undergo to gain a love that was otherwise unrequited," she murmured.

"You and she had history, Harper, but you always put Taylor's safety first. As a banshee, you all thought that Taylor was a threat, so perhaps she was willing to put her life on the line to encourage you to turn against her."

"But I didn't," Harper replied. "And Hunter wouldn't... we were never that serious."

"Never underestimate a woman scorned." Jenna smirked. "What did she fight you off with, Taylor? Some sort of knife?"

I frowned. "She had the hunter's dagger. The spelled hunter's dagger that... that I used to kill the last banshee with."

"Well then," she sighed. "It's just a theory, but let's just say that André declares that he would die for the panther. She makes the decision to die for Harper's love. You show up, willing to fulfil their dying wish, and she ambushes you. He comes to her rescue, in keeping true to his word, and he crosses over into the afterlife. Meanwhile, Harper stops her from killing you, and in doing so eliminates any hope that she had for reconciliation between the two of them... or perhaps she merely planned to die so Harper would kill you for taking his friend from him. But alas, Harper chose you, Taylor, so she chose to live for herself, or for her revenge, if the case may be."

Harper shook his head. "I've known Hunter for years, and me—"

"Girls aren't really that crazy-jealous are they?" Sal interrupted. "I mean, Wolfie isn't that—"

"It kind of makes sense." I shrugged. "I mean, it's a scary thought if it's true. I didn't think she hated me *that* much."

"It's just a theory," Harper mumbled. "The Hunter that I know wouldn't sink to that."

"Perhaps the Hunter now is not the Hunter that you once knew," Jenna replied. "It sounds as though her life has undergone a lot of changes in the past few months."

Harper shrugged. "All of our lives have."

"It's a nice story and all, but that doesn't help us save Taylor," Sal sighed.

"Maybe not," Jenna replied. "But it does help Taylor understand that what went on last Full Moon was not her fault. She was only carrying out her purpose. If she believes that taking André was a choice of hers, a choice that plagues on her mind, then she needs to let go of that guilt."

I scratched my eyebrow. "But it's just your theory, Jenna."

"Taylor Mistry," she said as she reached across and took my free hand in hers. "I am older than this city that you live in, and I have known banshees and other supernatural beings since the dawn of time. My theory about André and Hunter is just that, but trust me when I tell you that what I know of banshees is not just a theory. It is fact. Banshees do not hunt, they are not vindictive, they mourn death, and they assist the living into their eternal rest. *You* are not a monster, and neither is your nature, or *super*nature, as it were."

I drew in a breath and nodded. My gaze moved from her black eyes to Sal's orange eyes, then back to my favourite pair of olive-green eyes.

I didn't know what was coming, or who. I didn't know if I would be successful in my mission to stay alive or not. I didn't know what the future holds beyond the obstacles that I was currently facing. But I did know that whatever they were, I wouldn't face them alone. At the end of the day, I was surrounded by a group of friends that, despite how bleak things seemed, they were always there reminding me that no matter how isolated I felt sometimes, it was all an illusion. I was not invisible any more. I was not alone.

*

"It's Wednesday tomorrow. You have no classes," Harper said as he walked me to my door. We had stayed with Sal and Jenna until nightfall, and then all ended up having dinner together at *Clair de Lune*. It was spontaneous, but a surprisingly enjoyable evening. "Do you need to help at the veterinary clinic?"

I glanced at him. "I said that I would let them know if I could."

"Are you going to?"

"Do you want me to?"

He stopped and moved his hands to rest on my hips.

"I will not hold you back from doing the things that you want to do," he replied. "But I would like to be there if you choose to go."

I moved my arms around his neck. "I don't need to."

"But do you want to?"

"I want to figure out who left that note beside Theo," I sighed. "I want to felt safe again."

"Again?" He smiled. "Since I have known you, Taylor, you have been the most accident-prone person I have ever met."

I laughed. "I was framed."

He dipped his head to kiss my neck, then took my hand and guided me towards the door. I unlocked it to find Jesse and Brandon sitting on the couch. They looked up.

"Hello," Jesse said.

"Hey." Brandon smiled. He was playing with my cat, Raven.

"Hi." I nodded. "How's everything here?"

"Good," Brandon answered. "We were just planning your birthday party next weekend."

"Is it next weekend?"

Jesse sighed. "Next Sunday."

"Sunday." I frowned. The Full Moon. Perfect. "Um, Harper and I already have plans. We're, um, going away for the weekend."

Jesse's eyebrows lifted. "Oh."

"Sorry, I didn't know it was our birthday when I booked it."

Brandon pulled a face. "Can't you postpone?"

"The calendar is pretty set." I shrugged. "Why don't we do something, um, Friday night?"

"Why not Saturday?" Brandon asked.

"We will be away on Saturday too," Harper answered for me. "We leave Saturday morning."

Jesse nodded and stood up. "Friday night it is then."

"Where are you going, bro?" Brandon frowned. "It's quarter to ten at night."

"Work." My brother groaned. "Graveyard shift."

I nearly choked. "Jesse, you'll be careful right?"

"At work? Sure. It's a hospital." He shrugged, then leant over and kissed my cheek. "Good to see you again, sis. It's been ages."

My eyes rolled. "It's been, like, a day or two."

Jesse grinned. "I've still missed you. You're my other half."

"Love you too." I nodded.

He waved. "See you, Harper. Later, B."

"Bye, bro," Brandon called.

My brother left and I pressed my lips together.

"So, uh, Brandon, will you be staying here... in my house... again?" I asked.

He shrugged. "Maybe. Hey, did I hear that you lost that tooth necklace of yours?"

My eyebrows lifted. "Yes, why? Did you find it?"

Brandon lifted up Raven towards me. "There's one on your cat's collar."

"What?" I frowned. I stepped closer and then gasped as my breath caught in my throat.

"That's it, right?" Brandon asked. "It looks like it anyway."

I reached towards Raven. My hands shook as I unfastened the cord that had been tied beside her collar.

Brandon grinned. "Case solved."

I forced a smile that was filled with terror.

"Th-thanks," I said. I grabbed Harper's hand and dragged him towards my room. He looked a little confused but followed obediently. When we were both inside, I backed against my door.

"What's wrong?" he asked.

I held up the necklace. "Harper, this tooth is not a wolf tooth. It's a human tooth."

Harper frowned at it. "A canine. Theo's canine."

"They've been in my house," I mumbled. "They... Raven never goes outside, she's not allowed. She's too young. Harper—"

"Come on, grab your things we're going to my apartment," he replied.

I nodded and scrambled, shoving random items of clothing that were on my floor into the uni bag, which was still on my shoulder. I grabbed my toothbrush on the way out to leave. Harper was right behind me.

"Brandon, go home please," I said. "Just for tonight."

"Why?" He groaned. "What's up?"

I sighed. "Please don't argue with me. I'm not trying to be difficult. Jesse isn't here, and I'm staying with Harper so please just go home."

"What about the cat? She'll be lonely."

"She'll survive for one night." I shrugged.

Brandon frowned down at her and then stood. "I don't understand you, Taylor. But whatever."

I held out my hand. "Key."

"Why?"

"I don't want you letting yourself back in after I leave," I said. "It's for your own good, trust me."

Brandon grumbled a string of expletives. "I'd better get this back tomorrow, or I'll break in myself."

"Fine."

"Promise?"

I groaned. "Yes, I promise."

He put the key in my hand, and we all filed out the door. He muttered all the way to his silver ute.

"I might have just saved that idiot's life, and he's acting like an ungrateful jerk," I whispered.

Harper put my car into reverse. "I would have just left him there and let natural selection take its course."

"Harper!"

He smiled. "Kidding."

"No, you're not."

He chuckled and stepped on the accelerator.

"We should show the tooth to Cole," he said. "He might want to test it to confirm that it belongs to Theo and not someone else."

I shivered. "I know that this sounds horrible, but I hope it is Theo's. I don't want to think about someone else having their tooth pulled out."

Harper frowned, and I put my hand on his leg.

"What's wrong?"

He shot a quick glance in my direction. "If it is Theo's tooth, then it would confirm that the note was intended for you."

I nodded. "But... but we thought that was a possibility to begin with."

"Yes, but not a probability."

I bit my lip.

Cole wasn't home when we arrived back at the apartment building, but Harper called him. Within ten minutes, he had left Freeze Frame, where he had been working, and joined us in his lounge room. We hadn't seen the vampire for a few days, so after giving him the tooth to examine, I filled him in on the highlights, including the suspicious delivery of doughnuts to my unit.

"You don't know who sent them?" He frowned.

"No." I shrugged. "And Brandon ate them all, and there was nothing wrong with them."

"Curious."

I nodded. "Harper thinks it was strange that it was pastries that showed up. Any friend of mine wouldn't have sent something so unhealthy to me."

Cole thought for a moment, and then looked down at the tooth in his hands.

"This is a human tooth, and could very well be the same canine that Theo was missing," Cole replied. "I will need to get it genetically tested to be absolutely sure, but I would be quite confident in concluding that it belonged to him."

I didn't know whether to be relieved or not.

"It is also curious that whoever did this has made it into a necklace like the both of yours," Cole continued. "They would have to know that you wear one similar. There can't be too many people who know that."

I looked at Harper, and he wore the same concerned expression that I felt painted on my face. The grandfather clock began to chime for eleven o'clock, and I started at the noise. As it finished its interruption, the room fell silent again.

"Any ideas?" Cole asked.

We were all quiet for a moment, and then another ringing filled the room. I nearly jumped out of my skin until I realised that it was my phone. Harper and Cole watched me as I scrambled to answer it.

"Jesse," I muttered. "It's my brother. Hello? Jess?"

"*Taylor,*" he sighed. "*I'm glad that you're awake.*"

"What's wrong?"

"*It's April.*"

"April McKenzie?" I frowned. My former best friend who I'd had a fight with before my trip abroad to Italy. As a result, we lost touch while I was away, and when I got back, more had changed between us than just my appearance. I hadn't seen her in a couple of months. Not since Harper left and she and Ashley had attempted to get my mind off of it. Needless to say, our friendship fizzled out after that.

"*She's here,*" Jesse said.

I looked up at Harper and Cole who were both tipping their heads slightly to listen in.

"She's where?" I asked. I didn't think that Jesse would be home if he'd only started an hour ago, but I didn't want to go jumping to any unnecessary conclusions.

"*At the hospital. In the emergency department.*"

"Why?"

"*She was attacked by some kind of animal,*" he answered. "*It was pretty bad, Tay.*"

My hand covered my mouth. From my peripheral vision, I could see Harper and Cole exchange a look.

"How bad, Jesse?" I asked.

He sighed. "*She... she died, Taylor.*"

I pressed my fingers to my forehead. We may have parted on rocky terms, but I never would have wished her any harm.

We used to be close. She was one of my only friends for a long time.

"Was she alone?" I breathed.

If she was dying, then I knew that she wouldn't be completely alone. She would have had a reaper to relieve her from this mortal sphere.

"*I was here,*" he answered. "*Her brother is still out of town, but her parents are on their way.*"

April's brother, Louis, worked fly-in-fly-out. He was seven years older than her, than us, so although he'd been around when she was growing up, as soon as he was old enough, he began supporting himself. She often said that she wished that she and Louis had been closer in age so she could have something similar to what Jesse and I had. I think it was the only thing that she was jealous of me for.

Jesse and I were both silent, and then my brother sighed.

"*Listen, I've got to go, but I just thought you'd want to know,*" he finished.

"Thanks, um, thanks for telling me. For calling," I stuttered.

"*I'll see you later.*"

I exhaled. "Jesse, be careful, okay? Promise me that you'll be careful."

"*Yeah, I promise,*" he replied. "*You too.*"

"Yep."

The line went dead, and I stared at my handset then dropped it. Harper caught it before it reached the floor, and then wrapped his arms around me.

"I'm sorry about your friend," he sighed.

"She wasn't really... I don't understand," I mumbled. "An animal attack? That sounds—"

"Suspect," Cole said. "Indeed."

"But if someone was trying to get to me, why attack April? I wasn't even close to her any more. What was the point of hurting her?"

"You weren't close to Theo either," Harper replied. "But his death was sufficient in reaching you."

"Do you think that April was perhaps the *she* in *she's next?*" Cole asked. "Did April know Theo at all?"

I shrugged. "I haven't spoken to her in a couple of months. She could have known him, I suppose. I mean we all went to uni together, and she had slept with everyone... or a lot of guys. I shouldn't say that."

Cole looked back down at his phone as it buzzed. "It's Salvatore."

"Sal has your number?" I frowned.

Cole pressed a button on it and held the handset in the air.

"Salvatore," he said. "I'm here with Taylor and Harper. You're on speaker phone."

"*Good,*" Sal replied. "*Because someone else just died and I think that Taylor knows her.*"

"I do, it's April my... my old friend," I answered. "Jesse just called. It was an animal attack?"

"*Animal attack, right. It... it was bad. Like worse than Theo bad. She... it took a long time for her to die and it wasn't pretty. She had bite marks all down her leg and neck as if she'd been hunted down and then mauled.*"

I was about to tell Sal to spare the details until I realised that the devil was in the details.

"Was there anything else that you noticed, Salvatore?" Cole asked. "Anything that would link her to the wolf-hunter?"

"There was one thing that was weird," Sal said after a pause. *"I mean, apart from the fact that she was attacked out in the open."*

"What?" Harper near snapped. "What is it?"

"Well, she was covered in bites, and it looked like those are what made her bleed to death," Sal answered. *"But she only had one scratch on her. Or four, I guess, to her left shoulder, sort of like…"*

"Like mine," I breathed. My hand moved around to feel my scar. They were the only mark that I had on my body. They had been left by the banshee.

"Yeah, like Taylor's," Sal finished.

Harper pulled me closer against him.

"It's not a coincidence, is it?" I said. My voice sounded flat, dead. "Someone is definitely sending me a message."

Sal sighed. *"It… it sounds a little too coincidental for my liking."*

"Mine too," Harper growled.

"Salvatore, where are you now?" Cole asked.

"Home… well, uni," he answered. *"Why?"*

"Do you have a means of transport?"

"Nope, just my legs, Doc."

Cole nodded to himself. "Can you walk to Crescent? Ask Max, the bartender, to see Olivia Harrison."

"Oh… kay, who is Olivia Harrison?"

"It's Ruby's business alias," he replied. "She's there. It's student night. I'll call Ruby and tell her to expect you. Are you okay with that, Salvatore?"

215

"*Just call me Sal, Doc*," he answered. "*And it's cool. I'll head there now.*"

"Great," Cole sighed. "Be careful."

Phase Eight
The Trade

Cole hung up the phone and made his call to Ruby. It was super quick but, apparently, it only needed to be. As he began to pace, Lesleigh appeared in the doorway.

"Did I hear that someone was mauled by an animal?" she asked. "*Was* it an animal?"

"It seems so," Cole replied. "A vampire would not leave scratches, or require multiple entry points."

"Hm."

"What?" Harper asked.

Lesleigh's head tipped. "It just sounds sort of like something a werewolf would do, although it's not a Full Moon, so we can cross that animal out. What other species do we know that can transform without a Full Moon?"

"A shifter." Cole frowned. "A cat?"

"A jaguar panther, perhaps?" Lesleigh offered.

"Hunter," I whispered.

"Where is Hunter?" Harper asked. "Has anyone seen her since she got back?"

"No," Lesleigh replied. "She said that she had things to do. I haven't heard from her since."

"Has anyone?"

217

"Jenna has." I frowned. "Hunter attacked her when she was in raven form. She was the one that left that nasty scratch down her arm. I had to heal her before she, well, died, I guess."

Harper looked at me. "Where did this happen?"

I shrugged. "Jenna didn't say, but I found her in the courtyard outside my unit."

"You didn't tell me that," Harper murmured. "That she was wounded near your unit."

"What is it, Harper?" Cole asked. "Is that significant?"

"Jenna had this theory about Hunter," Harper explained. "That she intended to kill Taylor on the last Full Moon. She said that the reason why Taylor was called to her and André was that she was willing to die, to try to get me to turn against Taylor. I thought that it was ridiculous at the time but…"

"But?" Lesleigh prompted.

Harper glanced at her. "But Hunter would have no issues with killing a wolf-hunter. I know that, as she has done it before. She also knew about mine and Taylor's tooth pendant necklace, and would be fairly capable of breaking in to put this one on Taylor's *cat.*"

Cole looked at me warily.

"Hunter also knew about Taylor's aversion to sugary food and would use it as a taunt. Plus, she knew about April too. When I left Taylor for those weeks after the wendigo, I still kept surveillance on Taylor, and sometimes Hunter came along. She was there when you were out with April and Ashley, Taylor."

I sat down because I couldn't feel my legs any more.

"Hunter... could Hunter really do all of this?" I asked. "Do you think that she hates me... that she wants revenge on me that much?"

"If she believes that you took André and me from her, then who knows what she is capable of?" Harper answered. "Perhaps Jenna is right, and I underestimated her affection for me."

"*Dios mía*," Lesleigh groaned. "A woman scorned is the scariest creature of them all. A Spanish female were-panther scorned is not something I would want to be on the receiving end of."

"Thank you, Leigh, that is not helpful," Cole said curtly.

"Truth, Frost," she sighed. "I only speak it."

Harper sat down beside me and took my shaking hands.

"Cole, what are we going to do?" he asked. "We can't let her kill any more people."

"Well, first thing is first, we need to find her," Cole replied.

Harper leant back to take out his phone from his pocket. I watched as he scrolled through to find her number and hit the call button.

Cole moved his hands into his pockets. His brow was drawn, making his silver eyes darken as the shadows cast over them.

Lesleigh was looking around the room as if it had changed since she was there last, and she was trying to memorise it again.

After a moment, Harper shook his head and dropped his phone back into his lap.

"Nothing, she is not answering," he muttered.

There was a sound down the hallway, and we all looked up. It was Ruby and Sal. That was fast.

Ruby went straight over to stand beside Cole, and Sal stayed in the doorway.

"Taylor, Sal told me about your friend, I'm so sorry," Ruby said.

I nodded. "Thank you, though I hadn't seen her in a while."

"She was still your friend," Ruby replied. "I'm sure she knew how you felt about her. We all have friends that we can be separated from, but that doesn't mean... what?"

Harper, Cole, and I had exchanged an awkward look.

"Am I missing something?" Ruby asked.

Cole's eyes lowered. "We think that we know who is instigating everything. We believe that the same person who killed Theo also killed April."

Ruby looked at me, then back at her partner. "Who?"

"Hunter," Harper growled.

"Hunter? Our friend Hunter? Hunter Actaeon?" Ruby asked. "Do you think that she could really do something like this?"

"There are certainly several factors which indicate she is behind it," Cole said.

He went on to explain what we had deduced earlier, and I added in what Jenna had assumed with the odd interjection from Sal. After we had shared everything that we knew, Ruby shook her head.

"I just don't believe that she could—"

"I do," Lesleigh replied. "I've seen Hunter lash out before. It was in Spain, years ago, well before Harper's time. Cole had fled to Italy with Diana, but I was there with Miguel, and she completely lost the plot. She ripped into half a town over their beliefs on bullfighting. It was a complete blood bath. The only positive that came from it was that Miguel and I had a fresh meal for a change."

Sal made a face.

"Leigh, please," Cole sighed. "Edit yourself. We have company."

I rubbed my face, and Harper's hand moved to gently massage the base of my neck.

"We need to find her first," Ruby said. "Maybe then she can explain—"

"If she has done this, nothing that she says is going to suffice," Sal interrupted. "She has not only killed humans but tortured them. She made them suffer – she *wanted* them to suffer. She is a psychopath."

I looked up at Sal, and then lowered my head. As my eyes caught sight of my hands, I gasped.

"Oh no," I breathed.

"What is it?" Harper frowned.

"I… I'm… my glow," I stuttered. "It… it's so bright. Whatever we're doing, we're running out of time."

There was a sound at the door, and I jumped to my feet. Harper did the same.

"Who has access?" Lesleigh asked. "Cole."

"She's here," Harper sneered. "Hunter. I can smell her."

221

Slow footsteps echoed down the hallway, and then the Spanish beauty appeared. Her dark brown hair was wavy in tresses, wild, like the glint in her dark eyes. As she stepped through the door, the room shifted subtly. Cole stepped in front of Ruby, Harper moved in front of me, and Sal jumped behind Lesleigh. In Hunter's hands, she held two bags. One was black plastic and bulged, the other was fabric and slimline.

"Hunter," Cole said. "It is nice to see you. We were just talking about how long it has been."

Her black eyebrow lifted. "Well, well, I am glad you are all here. That does save me herding you all up."

"Why would you need to do that, Hunter?" Ruby asked as Cole's hand moved protectively in front of her. I wasn't sure what he thought Hunter could do to harm Ruby, or if she would even try, but it was clear that he wasn't taking chances where the love of his existence was concerned.

Hunter glanced at the two of them. "To make sure that no one tries to do anything heroic that may get anyone else killed."

"Hunter, what are you doing?" Harper asked. "What have you done?"

She glanced at him. "I'll be the one asking the questions, dear friend."

Her eyes moved from Harper to me, then narrowed.

"Hello, Banshee," Hunter taunted. "I have something of yours."

I glanced at her throat and swallowed. "You have my necklace."

"No, this is rightfully my necklace, I gave you the one that belongs to you," she replied. "Since you are as ruthless and murderous as the wolf-hunters are."

"I am not the one who killed two—"

"You killed André!" she roared. "I saw you."

I shook my head. "I didn't kill him, he wanted to die. Banshees just help those crossover—"

"Lies!" she snarled. "You are still the reason that he is dead."

I couldn't deny that. Whether the two of them wanted me there or not, I was there, and I helped him to die. It was fruitless in trying to get her to believe me because whatever way you looked at it, she was right. I had been the reason for his death.

"What do you have of mine?" I asked. "If not my necklace."

Her lips twisted. "I'll give you some clues, and you can guess."

Harper frowned. "Hunter—"

"Silence!" she snapped. "I am in control now."

I drew in a breath. "What are the clues?"

"All in good time." She smirked. "But first thing is first. Grim, make yourself useful."

She threw the black garbage bag in Sal's direction, and it fell to the floor with the sound of metal.

"What is that?" Lesleigh asked.

"That is for the grim to bind up you vampires," she said. "Move, Grim. *Now.*"

Sal stepped slowly out from behind Lesleigh and untied the bag. Inside was a collection of silver chains.

"This is mental," he mumbled. "You want me to chain them up? To what?"

Hunter sneered. "Use your imagination."

"That's really not necessary, Hunter," Cole said. "We're all friends here."

"But I can't have you interfering."

Lesleigh rolled her eyes and sat down at the table. Cole and Ruby walked over to do the same. I watched in horror as Sal very reluctantly removed the chains from the bag to fasten around their wrists. I could hear the burning it made against their skin. I stepped forward, but Harper pushed me back.

Hunter glanced over at us.

"Okay, Lovett, you have something of mine. The silver dagger, I want it back."

Harper frowned. "That was never yours."

"Well, I want it." She shrugged. "You have taken enough from me."

"What have I taken from you?"

"Everything," she growled. "You took everything from me, from the moment that you brought that... that *impotent girl* into our lives."

I heard Ruby whimper and looked back over as her head fell back, her eyes darkened to void blackness, and her teeth grew into fangs. I had never seen the vampires in their vampiric form before, but I assumed pain brought their predatory nature to the surface. I noticed that Cole and Lesleigh were in a little more control of themselves, as it was only their eyes that had changed. Control must come with age.

"Ruby, breathe through it," Cole whispered.

"I can't," she panted. "I can smell the blood. Sal needs to leave."

"No one is leaving," Hunter said. "Grim, fasten their feet too."

Cole frowned. "Hunter, I really—"

"Silence!" She scowled. "Banshee, you are with me."

I looked up. "Where are we going?"

"Nowhere, Taylor. I am just going to torture you until Harper gets me what I want."

Harper pushed me further back behind him.

"If you don't hand her over, then I will torture the grim instead, and he is not as durable to knives."

Sal looked over at me as he finished his job. I stepped around Harper.

"No, Taylor," Harper growled, and his hand caught my wrist.

"It's fine," I said. I leant over and kissed his parted lips. "I love you."

"Don't," he breathed.

I pulled his hand from my wrist and turned towards Hunter who was clenching her teeth. As I stepped towards her, she reached into the other bag in her hands. When I was two steps away, she flicked her wrist, and I felt pain tear through my side. I fell to my knees and reached to remove the knife. Hunter kicked my hand away.

"Leave it there," she hissed. "And Harper, every step that you take towards me, I'll put another one in her. Same goes for you, Grim."

I coughed. "I… I'm fine, stay there."

Hunter scoffed and knelt beside me. "Fine?"

I met her cold eyes and then felt another stab, this time in my thigh. I fell on my side and tried to push the black spots from my vision. I may not have been able to die from regular knives, but they still hurt as much if I was pierced with them. She must have known that I would heal if they were removed.

"Harper, *fetch* me the dagger," Hunter roared. "Or the banshee gets another one."

I tried to turn my head to see him, but the movement made the blades shift. I saw Hunter draw out another knife and noticed that each had their handles covered so that she could touch the silver without burning herself. I was just lucky, I guess, that silver wasn't toxic to me as it was most of the other supernatural beings that filled the room, all except Sal.

"I wonder if she will be able to breathe if I punctured her lungs," Hunter mused. "Not well, I imagine. How is this for a problem, Taylor? Are you re-thinking that whinge about food about now?"

"Stop, please stop," I sighed. "Harper, just get the dagger."

"She will kill you, Taylor," Harper answered.

I let out a whimper. "I'm already dead."

Hunter smiled a wicked smile and ran the point of the third knife alone my arm. I felt it tear my flesh and tried to hold in the cry.

"I… cannot… hear… you," she whispered into my face.

"Harper, go," I called.

I heard footsteps as the knife sank into my shoulder, and I felt my arm go numb. I let out a cry.

"Make it quick, Wolf," Sal yelled after him. "She can still bleed out on the floor."

Hunter drew another knife.

"Hunter, please," Cole said. I think that it was Cole. The voice was low and reasonable. "There is no reason to torture her."

"I can think of a few," Hunter replied. "Speaking of which, while we wait for Harper, let us start on those clues."

The knife sliced across my collarbone and I gritted my teeth.

"The first clue is that it is a *he*." She smirked and flicked the blade across my cheek. I flinched, and her black eyes twinkled. "The second is that he has a startling shade of blond hair."

He? Blond? Jesse? No. Not Jesse. Please, not Jesse.

Her fingers scrunched my hair, and she pulled on it, forcing my head back.

"Hunter, stop!" Lesleigh growled.

"Taylor!" Sal yelled.

Hunter's eyes looked up. "Careful, Grim, I have a whole bag of blades with her name on them."

I felt a tear trickle down the side of my face.

"What else?" Hunter mused. Her finger ran down my neck, and I felt a wet stickiness against my skin. I wondered how much more I could take before my body shut down. "Ah, he is tall. Six foot, perhaps."

I blinked to clear the moisture from my eyes. My mouth was dry. *No, Jesse.*

"And he has the most beautiful..." The tip of the knife sank into my stomach. "*Blue* eyes that I have ever seen."

Blue eyes. Not grey.

"Brandon," I mouthed. "You have Brandon?"

The blade went in deeper, and I screamed. She removed it and held it up in front of my face. I could see the blood dripping from the tip of it.

"He really is a dumb human." Hunter huffed. "Sweet, but stupid. It was too easy to lure him. Just one sight of a naked girl and he was eager to help."

I groaned internally, but I couldn't hold it against Brandon. Even though Hunter had been without clothes, it was probably chivalry that drove him to stop. Anyone would have done it. Hunter just underestimated humanity, or maybe she didn't, and she just relied on it.

"What do you want with him?" Sal asked. "Are you going to kill him too?"

Sal's question reminded me that Brandon must still be alive, or he would have otherwise been called away. A small part of me burst with relief.

Hunter's tanned shoulder lifted. "I may do, I may not. That depends entirely on Harper."

"Why him?"

Hunter's eyes narrowed. "Because, *Grim*, if he brings me the dagger, then I may just spare blondie's life."

"You just want the dagger? That's it?" Sal asked. "Then we can all go?"

She smiled and looked back to my exposed neck. She made another cut into it and looked back up at Sal.

"You can all go, I do not want anything from you," she replied. "As for Taylor, she owes me something, so when I get the dagger, I will be willing to make a trade."

"What trade?" Cole asked.

"Taylor's life for blondie's. He can live is she dies."

"And if she lives?" Lesleigh pressed. "Then what?"

Hunter let out a roar. "Then he dies, along with everyone else that Taylor has ever loved."

I closed my eyes.

"Taylor!" Sal called.

I opened them again and moved my hand. Before it got far, Hunter grabbed my wrist and thrust the fourth knife through it and into the floor. I let out a scream, and Hunter laughed.

"Sorry about your expensive floorboards, Cole," she said.

"Where in God's name is Harper?" Sal groaned.

I heard the front door close and whined in relief. His reappearance may mean that I'll die soon, but it couldn't be much worse than what Hunter was putting me through now. I couldn't understand why I wasn't passing out, but then I remembered that my body healed fast. I couldn't feel the first three knives that were still in me unless I moved. I must have healed around them.

I heard Harper string a bunch of French words together.

"Hunter, what the hell are you doing?" he growled.

"Easy, Lovett," she taunted. "Stay where you are."

"Did you get the dagger?" Sal asked.

229

"Yes, I have it," Harper replied. "So you can let her go now, Hunter."

She roared with laughter.

"She's not letting Taylor go," Sal said. He spoke quickly. "She has Brandon, and she'll kill him and everyone else that Taylor knows unless she kills Taylor."

"Where are you keeping Brandon, Hunter?" Cole asked.

Hunter looked up, and I took the distraction to try to move the fingers of the hand that was nailed to the floor. I felt them twitch, but it hurt to move them.

"Give me the dagger, Lovett, and I just might tell you where blondie is," she answered. "No one else has to die… except for Taylor that is."

"Harper just do it," I mumbled. I was tired. I just wanted it to end.

"Tell us where he is first," Harper said.

"Are you crazy?" Sal shrieked. "You're not giving her the dagger, are you? She'll kill Taylor!"

"Lovett!" Hunter snarled, extending her hand.

"Harper, don't."

"Silence, Reaper," Harper barked. "Tell us, Hunter."

"Give me the dagger, Lovett," Hunter answered. I saw her hand move for another knife.

I whimpered. "Harper, please, just give it to her. I love you, just do what she says."

I saw Hunter reach for something, and then she rocked back. She smiled at the silver dagger in her hands, and then looked down at me.

"He is…" Hunter said. She lifted the dagger above me. "I'll never tell."

Her hand fell, and I gasped as the blade sank through my chest.

The air gurgled in my throat.

The black spots in my vision won.

*

"Give her some room," Cole's voice said. "Taylor. Taylor, can you hear me?"

I thought I was dead. Why was I not dead?

"Harper?" I murmured. "Harper."

"Taylor, I am here," Harper said. I felt a pressure on my hand. But wasn't that hand pinned to the floor?

I opened my eyes, and instead of black spots, I saw bright blurs. As I blinked, the mistiness began to clear.

"Harper," I breathed. "I love you."

His light green eyes were big and bright. "I love you too, to the Moon and back."

I smiled. "Why aren't I dead? Where is Hunter?"

"Taylor Mistry," Jenna's voice said. Her face appeared across my vision. "Welcome back."

My free hand lifted, and I felt my chest and found no gaping hole in it. There was a hole in my top though, and my clothes felt sticky, but everything seemed intact. I tried to sit and slipped in the blood that I lay in. It looked as if someone had tried to clean it up around me.

"Careful," Harper whispered. "Slowly."

My body felt stiff as I rolled up. The other knives that had been stuck into me were lying beside me. It was somewhat of a relief to know that I hadn't dreamt it all, but that didn't make it any of it less confusing.

"What happened?" I asked. "Where is Hunter?"

Harper looked behind me, and I followed his gaze to the table. She was bound to one of the chairs with the silver chains that had been used to fasten the vampires. Instead of just her hands though, her entire body was wrapped in them. Her mouth was covered with electric tape.

"That was my touch." Sal smiled. "I didn't want to take any chances, you know?"

"Why is she still alive?" I asked. I looked back to Harper. "I thought you would have killed her already."

He nodded. "I wanted to, but Cole wouldn't let me until we found out where she was keeping Brandon."

"Brandon," I sighed. "She hasn't said?"

"Not yet," Harper growled.

I drew in a breath, and my hand lifted to my chest. It still felt a little tender.

"Why didn't the silver dagger kill me?" I asked. "It should have killed me."

Harper looked up at Jenna. "It should have… if it was the right dagger."

I looked up at them. "What do you mean?"

"Harper took it upon himself to make a wish on your behalf," she said. "He wished for a silver replica of the dagger without the magical means to kill a banshee. He was very specific."

I frowned. "How did he find you?"

"Cole was kind enough to offer me shelter on one of the lower levels," she answered. "He came to me after he'd retrieved the real dagger."

Sal lifted it up, and I looked over. For some reason, I felt like crying, so I did.

"Taylor," Harper sighed. "It's okay, you're safe now."

I shook my head. "This is all such a mess. I never meant for anyone to get hurt because of me, and now two people are dead, and Brandon—"

"We will find him," Harper said. "Lesleigh is already looking."

I sniffled and looked around. "Where is Ruby?"

"Resting." Cole frowned. "The silver affected her more than Leigh and I."

"Will she be okay?"

"Yes. She just needs to get her strength back. It's nothing that a lot of blood and a cold bath won't fix. Speaking of…" He lifted a metal cup towards me. "Drink this."

I took it. "What is it?"

"Colloidal silver. It will help you heal."

I drank the liquid as quickly as I could and felt the effect instantly in my body.

"Better?" Harper asked.

I nodded. "I'd like to try to stand."

"Are you sure? Be careful, it… it's slippery."

Jenna took the cup from my hands, and I began to push myself up. Harper gripped my arms and bore most of my weight. My body hurt more as my muscles tensed and I straightened. Regardless, the pain wasn't nearly as bad as I had just endured.

"Okay?" Harper frowned.

I swayed a little, so clung onto him.

"Yes," I sighed. "Where is Lesleigh looking?"

"She was going to start at Hunter's cabin," Harper said.

I shook my head. "That's too far away. Brandon was driving from my house, remember? He was headed south into South Coast. That's where he lives. Lesleigh needs to look around there. Try the cemetery, and around the university. She had to have been back at the esplanade to attack April, so he must be close to there."

Harper looked at Cole, and Cole nodded.

Sal slid off the chair beside Hunter.

"How are you feeling, Mistry?" Sal asked. "I'm sorry I didn't do anything when that bitch was stabbing you."

Hunter fought against the chains. I glanced over and remembered that I had called her a *bitch* once. She had rebuked me saying that she 'was no dog'.

"That's okay, Sal," I said. "You did the right thing. She would have only hurt me more, or worse, hurt you instead."

Sal nodded, but he still looked like he was wrestling with his better judgement.

"Seriously, don't beat yourself up," I sighed. "I'm okay now. I'm feeling a lot better."

He pressed his lips together. "How's the glow?"

Harper focused back on me, and I looked down. I hadn't thought to check since awakening, I'd had so many other things to think about.

"It's almost completely gone." I exhaled. "I guess the threat of my death has been neutralised."

Sal looked over at Hunter, and then smiled back at me.

"Lesleigh is going to check by the university," Cole said. "Then she'll head to the cemetery and check there."

"Can't we go there?" I asked. "I want to help. I don't want Sal to be the one to find him first."

Sal looked confused, and then comprehension hit. "Oh. Yeah, that's—"

He stopped talking suddenly, and Cole, Harper, and I exchanged a look. Jenna frowned and Hunter's black eyebrows lifted.

"Crap," Sal sighed. "I've got to go."

"No," I breathed. "You can't."

"If I stay, it won't make whoever it is live longer, it'll just make them suffer longer," Sal replied.

I gritted my teeth and looked at Hunter who appeared to be smiling under the electric tape.

"Take me with you, Sal," I said. "I'll go there with you then see where it is, then I'll let go."

Sal made a face. "That's a terrible idea. Do you remember what happened the last time you did that?"

I bit my lip. The last time I had tried to jump in with Sal was on Ashley's death. It resulted with me being pushed back to where I was as if I had been thrown from the eye of a cyclone back down to earth. I had smashed into a headstone and crumbled it. My only saving grace was that I was also transforming into the white woman, a full banshee. It was the last Full Moon.

"I have to try. Sal, I can't let him die."

Sal shook his head. "*If* it is him, he's already dying. You can't stop that, regardless."

"I have to try."

"Taylor, you might not be strong enough," Cole reminded me. I hated that it was coming from him because he was the only one that I would have believed. He was a doctor of humans and an authority on the supernatural.

"Let her go," Jenna said. "She might be able to do it."

Sal rolled his orange eyes and extended his hand towards me. I kissed Harper's and then grabbed it. The next moment I was being sucked through a vortex and the crisp surroundings of Cole's apartment faded into dirty bricks. I yawned to pop my ears, and then realised where I was.

"This is my unit." I frowned.

At first, my stomach lurched. What if it was Jesse who was dying and Hunter was messing with me yet again? After all, grey eyes could look blue. I had often thought that Jesse sometimes looked like he had pale blue eyes rather than grey.

"Taylor," Sal whispered.

I turned and saw legs coming out from behind my two bins, which were tucked in the corner of my front courtyard. I gasped and let go of Sal's hand, but instead of being thrown back into Cole's apartment, I was flung back against the wall of my house. I crunched my back and then shook it off, running over to the body that was either my brother or his best friend.

I exhaled when I knelt by Brandon's feet.

"Hey, Brandon," I said. "Wake up."

He had a massive gash on his head that had been bleeding pretty severely. There was also blood on his shirt, which could have dripped from the head laceration, or come from somewhere else. I looked around for anything to clot it with, and then groaned and pulled off my own top. As a general rule, I never undressed in public, ever. Even when I'd lost the weight, I had been self-conscious, since I still had a little bit of padding left around my middle that I couldn't shake. Plus, the stretchmarks made it look like I had been attacked by a wildcat. But this was somewhat of an emergency, and the bleeding needed to be stopped. I pressed the shirt to Brandon's head and felt around his legs. They didn't seem to be harmed, so I climbed gently over to get a better angle at his head. My shoes slipped in blood that had pooled beside him. It was lucky that I wasn't squeamish around blood, since tonight, I had seen enough to last me a lifetime.

"Brandon," I said. "Brandon, it's Taylor, can you hear me?"

I knew the lack of consciousness could have nothing to do with the blood loss – shock could also cause people to pass out. He could also drift in and out of consciousness. I was just clinging to any signs that he wasn't as bad as he looked.

I pressed my free hand to his chest, but couldn't feel anything. If he had a heartbeat, it was very weak. I looked around for his hand and found it bathing in the blood beside him. My fingers felt for the inside of his wrist.

"Brandon Hadley."

As I furiously felt for a pulse, I leant in to feel if he was even breathing. There was slight warmth, but it wasn't enough to give me hope. I finally found a pulse inside his wrist, but it was barely there. I clenched my teeth and glanced over my shoulder to see if Sal was still here. I couldn't see him if he was.

"Sal, if you're here, go back and tell Cole where we are. Tell him to bring type O Rh D negative blood."

I felt like I was talking to myself, but I didn't care. I wasn't going to give up easily. Hunter wouldn't win.

I unravelled my top and tied it around the cut on his head to free up my hands, and turned my attention back to his windpipe to make sure that the passage was clear. I would have probably tried to lie him down, but I was mindful not to move him since I didn't know the extent of his other injuries. My first aid knowledge told me that since he had a head injury, he could also have damaged his spine and neck.

I tipped his head carefully back and held it steady there. I didn't know how long it was sustainable for me to keep him in that position, I just hoped that Sal would call someone for help soon.

So far, there was no clear fluid leaking from his ears or nose, which was a good sign. My father had taught me that if there was, it could indicate a skull fracture. Around his eyes appeared to be a little dark, which could mean that the blow to his head was hard enough to rupture blood vessels in or around them. I carefully lifted myself to my knees and moved my hand to his cheek. I put pressure on my fingers to pry his eyes open. There didn't seem to be any discolouration or bleeding in the whites of his eye. I took that as a small victory, considering the lighting was terrible out here.

I sank back to sit, careful not to put too much weight on his legs as to cut off circulation and looked down at the blood on his abdomen. I moved one of my hands under his chin to keep his head tilted, since that seemed to help him to breathe, and then pulled up the bottom of his T-shirt.

"Crap," I groaned.

It looked as if he'd been stabbed with something just below the ribcage. I didn't want to inspect the wound too much, since removing the fabric had torn the makeshift clot. I pressed my hand to apply pressure on the injury to plug it and felt Brandon flinch.

"Brandon, can you hear me?"

His eyes worked to open.

"Brandon," I said again. This time louder.

He exhaled. "Mm."

"Brandon, its Taylor. Don't try to move, okay? You're hurt."

"Tay… Taylor." He choked and lifted his own head. I steadied it in my hand and wiped the blood from his eyebrow. His blue eyes tried to find me in the shadows.

"Hey," I sighed. "You scared the life out of me."

"My head…" he muttered. He tried to lift his hand and then dropped it again.

"I said not to move, you numpty."

His eyes struggled to stay open, but his mouth tried to smile.

"You're my biggest…" he murmured.

"What?" I frowned. "Brandon, don't try to talk."

He moaned. "No."

239

Where the heck was Sal?

"Taylor," he breathed.

"Shh, shut up, Brandon." I swallowed. I could feel the blood pulsing through my fingers from his abdomen. "For once, just shut up."

He tried to laugh but cringed. "You're my biggest regret."

I frowned at him as his eyes slipped back closed.

"Brandon," I said. His head fell back. "Brandon Hadley, open your eyes. Brandon."

I heard car tires skid to a stop and exhaled.

"Help!" I called.

"Taylor?"

"In here, hurry," I said. I nearly started crying with relief.

Cole kicked the bins back with his feet to get better access.

"Status?" he asked, shrugging out of his waistcoat.

"He has a laceration to his left temple and what looks like a stab wound to the right side of his abdomen, just below his ribs. I'm not sure about anything else, but he was unconscious when I found him; he was alert for a couple of seconds, but seems to have lost consciousness again."

Cole dropped his waistcoat over my bare shoulders. "Did he move his head when he was alert?"

"Yes, yes he could, he did." I nodded.

"You've done well, Taylor," Cole replied. "He's hanging on, but only just. I'm going to need to take it from here."

"Cole, if I move my hand, he'll bleed more." I blinked. "He can't die. You have to save him."

Cole nodded and opened his medical kit. "I'll do my best."

I looked back and saw Sal lingering under the light. Cole moved his hand close to mine.

"Taylor, when I say so, I need you to remove your hand and move clear of him as carefully as possible. Can you do that for me?"

I swallowed. "Yes."

"Salvatore… Sal," Cole said. "Come and help Taylor to stand, her legs might be unsteady. Lift her by the armpits and then take her to get cleaned up."

I was too scared to argue, even if I wanted to stay and help him with Brandon.

Sal stepped in behind me and clutched my shoulders.

"On three," Cole sighed. "One, two, three."

There was hardly a pause between the numbers, and then everyone was moving like clockwork. Sal lifted me up as I pushed off the bricks, and Cole swooped under to start on Brandon. I could hardly make out what he was doing since he appeared to be moving very quickly. But then again, I was also busy stumbling over Sal.

"Thank goodness you heard me," I sighed. "I was scared that you were lurking around waiting for him to flat-line."

Sal helped me stand, and then frowned at me.

"Heard you?" he asked. "What are you talking about, Mistry? The moment you let go of me and launched yourself at the guy, I went back to Cole's apartment and told them where you were."

"Oh." I frowned. So I *was* talking to myself.

Sal opened my front door. I wasn't sure how, but then I saw he had my key in his hand. It confused me, but I went along with it. The blood I was covered in was making my stomach turn.

"It was weird though," Sal continued. "As soon as you let go, it sort of felt like I didn't need to be here any more. You must've really known what you're doing."

I shrugged. I felt a little dazed, so I leant against his shoulder. I pointed toward the bathroom, and he guided me there. When we were through the door, I found the edge of the bath to sit on.

"Well, my dad taught me first aid and... and he is a neurosurgeon, so I know a little. Plus, I used to test Jesse on medical stuff sometimes."

"There are a lot of Mistrys in medicine."

I smiled weakly, and my eyes began to droop. "But I prefer animals though."

Sal smirked. "I guess that's why Harper is your perfect man."

"That... he is," I sighed. I reached for the tap and began turning them until the water that wasn't cold or hot began to fall into the recess.

Sal bit down on his lip. "Taylor, there was something that I wanted to talk to you about."

"Is this going to be awkward? Because I've been through enough tonight without adding an awkward conversation to it."

He laughed. "Not too awkward in the scale of awkwardness."

"Okay," I said. "What's on your mind then?"

"I thought that you could use one of your wishes to wish that we traded jobs," he replied. "You know, so you're a reaper, and I'll be a banshee instead."

I blinked slowly. "You want to be a screaming white woman?"

"Don't be sexist."

"I'm not, but that's what banshees usually are."

He shrugged. "And reapers are usually guys. But regardless, we can take some liberties if we have a djinn orchestrating it."

"Sal, why are you suggesting that we trade?"

He frowned. "Because I don't want you to die, Taylor. Not tonight, and not ten years from now. I want you to be able to live for as long as you want with your werewolf boyfriend and not have to worry that you have a time limit hanging over you."

"And what about you?"

"What about me?" he asked. "I should have died years ago, but fate smiled on me."

"I should have died too, you know. At least four times. Probably more by now."

He tipped my chin up. "Well, what's another smile from fate then? I just want you and Wolfie to have a very dull life together."

I smiled weakly. "That's sweet."

He laughed.

My hand lifted to my chest. "Sal?"

"Yes?"

"Where is Harper?"

Sal frowned. "He's at the apartment where we left him. Hey, are you okay? You look weird."

My head nodded and shook at the same time.

"I just... my chest feels a little tight," I gasped. "Did you say that he... he... you left him with... with Hunter? Are they alone?"

"Taylor, what's going on?" he asked. "Are you okay? Should I get—?"

"No." I choked. "No, I... I just... I—"

The air was sucked from my body like a vacuum. I tried to grip onto the acrylic of the bath, but the blood still on my hands made them slip. Sal knelt before me and reached for my hand, so I clutched him instead.

"What can I do?" he asked. "Taylor, please—"

My forehead creased and I squeezed his hand harder as the wrenching sensation rippled through my body from the tips of my toes all the way to the top of my head.

"Taylor!" Sal exclaimed urgently.

My eyes seemed to glaze over.

"Such is fate," I murmured, and then I let out the most bloodcurdling scream that had ever been heard.

Epilogue
Para Normal

"Tay, hey, sleepy," a voice whispered. "Wake up."

I stirred and then groaned.

Someone poked my cheek. "Taylor Maye, open your eyes."

I smacked the hand. "Go away, Jesse Jay."

"You can't tell me what to do. It's my birthday."

My eye opened and exhaled. "Well, it's mine too."

Jesse chuckled. "Happy birthday, sis."

"You too, Jess."

He collapsed on me and awkwardly moved his arms around me. "Twenty-two sucked. I'm glad it's over."

"Amen to that," I sighed. "This year had better be *exceedingly* uneventful."

Jesse sat back and nodded. "So what are you doing today?"

I sat up. "I think Ruby was going to take me out somewhere. What about you?"

"Not sure. Brandon is keen to get drunk, but he's still on his meds so I'll probably need to babysit him."

I smiled to myself. Brandon had been lucky that Cole had arrived when he did. I wished that I could have seen him work his medical magic to save his life, but I was too busy wailing over the death of…

"I don't really feel much like celebrating anyway," Jesse added. "I suppose you don't either."

My eyes lowered. "No, not especially. So what's going on between you and Amelia?"

"Nothing." He shrugged. "I told her that I wasn't ready for anything."

"Why?"

"Because I'm not, Tay. Not yet."

"But you can still be friends, can't you?"

"I don't want to make things harder for her," Jesse said. "I shouldn't have started anything with her. She deserves more, and that's something I can't give her right now."

"You actually really like her, don't you?"

He smiled weakly. "Right now is not our time. But maybe one day it will be. It's not fair to her when I'm still getting over... over Ashley."

"But now she's grieving over April," I said. "You should be there for her. She was there for you."

"I'm not who she needs. If I were around, then it would only complicate things for her. She needs to be around family and her other friends now."

"Her brother moved away," I reminded him. "And her friend just died. I don't remember seeing her photographed with anyone besides Marcus, so if you want to talk about complicated, then there it is."

Jesse sighed. "So are you all cleared out?"

I gave up on the topic and looked around my room, which was emptied of everything except the bed.

"Yes, almost," I replied.

"It's convenient that Brandon's injuries mean that he couldn't help with the moving."

"Oh, I'm sure he meant to get carjacked and attacked for the express purpose of not being able to help with a move that he didn't even know about at the time." I nodded. "Sneaky bastard."

Jesse smirked. "You'll still visit though, right?"

I rolled my eyes. "Jess, I'm moving across the river, not across the country. Of course I'll still visit."

"Good," he sighed. "You can treat this place the way you always have. Only this time you can't actually ask Brandon to leave since, you know, he'll *actually* live here."

I huffed. After the whole ordeal of last Tuesday evening, I had decided that it was best to separate myself a little from my human family and friends and move into Cole's apartment building. It suited everyone really since Brandon would actually acquire a bed here, and Cole had most of his building sitting vacant.

"True." I nodded. "Just make sure you don't forget to feed Raven."

"Are you sure you don't want to take her? She is your cat."

I pressed my lips into a smile. "Sure, I'm sure. She's used to the place here, and Brandon loves her. Plus, I can't have pets in the apartment block."

I didn't want to add that seeing the black cat just reminded me of a miniature version of Hunter. Even just thinking about the were-panther set off the pain centre in my brain. There were a lot of reasons why I couldn't allow myself to dwell on her.

There was a knock at the front door, and I looked in the direction of it.

"I'll get it." Jesse smiled. "You get dressed."

"Thanks," I sighed. "Love you, Jess."

"Love you too."

He slipped out my door and closed it. I poured myself out of bed and pulled on the only clothes that I hadn't already moved over. I seemed to have about the same amount of things to move from here as I did to move here – and that wasn't much at all.

I stopped in at the bathroom to brush my teeth on the way out to Jesse and our company. For the past week and a half, whenever I was in here, I had to close my eyes. I couldn't allow myself to think of that night. I didn't know how Jesse could still live in the unit after what had happened to Ashley here when nothing had *physically* happened to me here. I looked down and spotted a tile with bloodstained grout down the edge of the bath, and leant over to scratch away the mark. Apparently, Sal had missed it when he cleared the smears that I had left in my haste to leave.

I washed my hands clean and then dropped my toothbrush back into my toiletry bag, ready to bring it with me. I returned to my room, my old room, and jammed the bag into my backpack with my pyjamas, and headed out.

"Good morning, Taylor." Ruby smiled. "Are you ready?"

I nodded and glanced at Brandon who was still asleep on the couch. Raven was curled up around his head.

"Will you be okay, Jesse?" I asked. "You will be, won't you?"

He smiled. "Yes. Yeah, I'll be fine. You don't have to worry about me, Taylor."

I bit my lip and walked over to him, giving him a proper hug for the first time on our twenty-third anniversary together on the planet. For some reason, it felt like it could be the last one too.

"I love you more than my own life," I said.

"That's a little dramatic." He chuckled. "But you know that I feel the same."

I stepped back and exhaled.

"Are you two staying for breakfast, or do you have to leave now?" he asked.

"We were going to get an early start," I replied. "If that's okay."

"Tay, you don't have to clear anything with me, seriously." Jesse laughed. "Go, enjoy your day."

I nodded. "You too."

He waved weakly, and I started towards the door. I stopped by the table and slid my key onto the edge of it.

"You keep that," Jesse said. He rolled his grey eyes. "Knowing Brandon, he'll lose his, and it's better to have a third party with a copy."

"Okay, thanks."

"See you, Taylor."

"Goodbye, Jesse," I whispered.

He smiled, but there was a hint of sadness in it. I wondered if that's what he saw when he looked at me too.

Ruby led the way to Cole's black Jag and opened the door for me. I dropped my backpack in and slid into the passenger seat. Ruby sat behind the steering wheel then looked over at me.

"Happy birthday, Taylor." She grinned. "What's it like being twenty-three?"

Twenty-three. I honestly never thought that I'd make it.

I shrugged. "Just like twenty-two."

Ruby pressed her lips together. "And what was twenty-two like?"

"Just like twenty-one, but with more death," I replied, and then laughed. "Well, for me at least."

Being a vampire, Ruby had technically frozen in aging at twenty-one. At least as a banshee, my body was still alive for all intents and purposes.

"I do hope that this year is less eventful for you," she sighed, starting the car engine. "You have been through a lot... lost a lot too."

I nodded. Although I had achieved my weight loss goal within the last year, that seemed like another lifetime ago now. I knew that Ruby hadn't been referring to my weight loss though. I'd lost so much more than that: friends, enemies, normality, faith...

"But I've gained a lot too," I murmured. "New friends, well, new family really, and love."

"Love." She nodded.

Harper.

"You miss him," she whispered.

"I always miss him. Even when he's with me, I miss him, because I know that there would come a time when he won't be with me."

She glanced over at me. "I know how you feel."

"But Cole is there for you all the time, whenever you need."

"Harper is with you too, even if you can't see him," she said. "He's in your thoughts, your heart. He'll never really be gone."

I sighed and studied my torn cuticles. I tended to pick at my nails when I was anxious. I hadn't realised that I had been, but I guess it was expected after everything. I turned my hand over and studied my palm. The glow that I had once seen around me had all but faded to nothing. It was a relief in a lot of ways, but it felt like a dormant landmine in a lot of others.

Ruby made a left turn, and I looked up.

"Where are we going?" I frowned. It wasn't quite in the direction of the apartment block where we both now lived.

"It's a surprise," she answered.

Even as a vampire slash former lawyer, Ruby was rubbish at lying.

"The cemetery?" I sighed. "I don't want to go there."

"Sure you do."

I rested my head back. "Well, it's not like I really have a choice anyway."

"Exactly." She laughed. "So at least try and pretend to be excited."

"About the cemetery?"

"Yes."

I forced a tight smile, and she chuckled.

"That's the spirit," she said.

I rolled my eyes.

It only took four more turns until we were pulling into the narrow streets of the buried deceased and then two more until we were pulling up alongside a familiar landmark. The Amund Tomb.

"What are we doing here, Ruby?" I asked.

"Paying our respects," she said. She opened her door and climbed out.

I exhaled and did the same. "Paying our respects to whom?"

"To you." She shrugged.

A chorus of 'surprise' sounded, and three other different types of mystical beings jumped out at us.

I could see only one.

"Harper," I breathed. I ran straight to him and into his waiting arms. "You're here."

"Of course I'm here. I couldn't miss your birthday."

I squeezed him as tightly as I could and heard him yelp.

"I'm so glad that you're here," I whispered. I could feel the tears form in my eyes. "But what about the Moon?"

"What about the Moon?" He shrugged. "As far as I'm concerned, the world can wait."

I hugged him again.

"Hello? What about the rest of us?" Sal groaned. "Clearly, Taylor Maye Mistry, your manners have not improved with your age."

"Oh, let them be," Jenna sighed. "They're in love."

I looked up and smiled. "Hello, Jenna, Sal. Cole, it's nice to see you."

"And you, Taylor." Cole nodded. "Happy birthday."

"Thanks, it is now."

Harper kissed my head.

"So, this is great and all, but I was kind of hoping for breakfast," I sighed. "Did anyone think to bring any food?"

The five of them exchanged a look.

"Really?" I frowned. "You threw me a makeshift surprise party in a cemetery and didn't even bring me any cake? What is wrong with you people?"

"Well, to be fair, almost half of us survive on a liquid diet," Ruby replied.

I tipped my head and looked to Sal. "So what's your excuse?"

He shrugged. "I ate it all on the way?"

Jenna pressed her lips together. "Do you… wish… you had some food, Taylor?"

"Well, sure," I answered. "I guess."

Jenna lifted her scarred hand and clicked her fingers, and a banquet appeared on tables between the car and tomb.

"Well, hell yes, Taylor Maye, nice way to use your second wish!" Sal exclaimed.

Second.

Because Harper had made the first wish on my behalf to ensure I wasn't killed last Tuesday when I was being tortured. It's incredible the difference a plain silver dagger made in comparison to one that had been melted and set by two usually opposing forces, the Shadow Weavers and the Light Lacers. That little technicality had saved my life.

It wasn't one that would save a cat-shifter's life though.

Any kind of silver that was forced into her beating heart would poison her blood, sending toxicity through her internal system, and stun it into death. Or so I'm told.

Harper and I had an unspoken rule that we didn't talk about his former friend. Her name hadn't been mentioned since last Wednesday morning when we were still cleaning up the chaos that she had bestowed upon us all.

Finding Brandon, getting cleaned up, feeling breathless, the scream...

"Something's wrong," I'd breathed after wailing. *"Sal, I need you to call Harper now."*

"Why? Do you think that's what the scream—?"

"Just do it. I need to make sure that he's okay."

Sal scrambled for his phone. I extended my hand towards it, and he put it in my palm. I waited while it rang and then suppressed a sob as it went to Harper's generic answering machine message.

"Call it again." I said.

"Taylor, I—"

"I said to call it again, Salvatore!"

I twisted to turn off the tap behind me and drew in a breath. Sal dialled and put it on speakerphone. Hearing the echoes of it ringing aloud and unanswered was almost as painful as Hunter's knives had been.

"Grim?" Harper's voice resounded. *"Is Taylor all right?"*

"Harper." I exhaled. *"What happened... what? Are you all right?"*

There was a short silence, and I wondered if the call had been disconnected.

"Hunter is dead."

I drew in a breath and ignored the immense relief that I felt, knowing that my torturer wouldn't see another sunrise.

"Are you okay?" I breathed.

"Yes."

"Harper?"

"It had to be done, Taylor."

I looked at Sal, and he seemed as unapologetic about the news as Harper sounded.

Sal lifted a shoulder. *"Que Será."*

I bit my lip. *"Is everyone else okay?"*

"Yes. Is Brandon?"

"Cole is with him," I sighed, then sniffled. *"He was really bad, Harper. Really bad."*

"He will be okay, Taylor."

My head shook. *"This is my fault."*

"No," Harper and Sal replied in unison.

"She would have never gone after him, or April, or even Theo if it wasn't for me."

Sal tipped his head. *"Well, Theo wasn't really—"*

"I can't be around them. I can't do it. Being what I am puts them in danger, if not from me, then from someone that's after me."

Harper exhaled. *"You are not the problem. Taylor, I won't let anyone—"*

"But they already have," I answered. *"Harper, I need... I want to live with you, in your apartment. If... if that's okay. Maybe if we're—"*

"Yes," he replied. *"Of course, Taylor. Move in tomorrow, today. Right now even."*

And that was all that was said on the matter.

I hadn't heard her name out loud since, though, it had echoed in my mind, my memories, and my nightmares frequently for the first few days after.

Harper never went into detail about the way in which she was killed, but judging by the number of bloodstains in the lounge room of Cole and Ruby's apartment, it wasn't pleasant.

I never asked.

I didn't want to know, and I was sure that Harper didn't want to talk about how his closest friend and confidante had betrayed him and tormented me.

I never wanted it to end this way.

As much as the were-panther and I had clashed, I knew how important she had been to Harper. She had been important to Cole and Lesleigh too. But she had decided that, for some reason, vengeance was more important than friendship. Rage and revenge took precedence over loyalty, and now, despite our varying opinions of her, we were all worse off because of it.

Jenna stepped forward and extended a muffin towards me.

"Low fat berry-muesli." She smiled proudly.

Jenna and I had become close over the past week. In fact, we had all pulled together after what had happened. I'd never had so many friends before, especially some that had continually put themselves in harm's way to get me out of it. They were there for me just because they wanted to be there, and not because they wanted to be in Jesse's good graces.

We may be a strange bunch of mismatched mystical creatures, but together, we were stronger than when we were apart. I would never be alone, and I could never feel lonely when I was surrounded by people who never looked through me, but saw me for who I was—who I've always been, flaws and all—and liked me even more for it.

"Taylor Mistry, you still have one more wish left," Jenna said. "So what is it going to be?"

"I've thought about it, and I've decided that I don't want it," I replied.

Jenna smiled, and I looked around the circle at my friends, and rolled my eyes at Sal who was trying to fit an entire slice of my white-chocolate mud cake into his mouth. He ended up with a massive smear of light-green icing over his face.

"I've already got everything that I'll ever want," I added. "Everything I could ever need is right here."

Jenna breathed a laugh, and her dark eyes glittered in the morning sun.

"You are still very odd, Taylor Mistry," she said.

"Crazy is what she is." Sal huffed. "Wish for more cake."

Ruby shook her head, but the others just ignored Sal's comment. We were all getting pretty good at it.

"Taylor's not crazy." Ruby smiled, and her hand found Cole's. "She's just grateful."

Cole kissed her head, and I glanced up at Harper.

"That." I nodded. "And I suppose I just trust in fate."

"Fate," Harper replied. "Love."

He wound his arms around me, binding our bodies together as his hands gently tipped my lips towards his. He smiled, and his nose brushed mine.

"Such is fate," he whispered.

I lifted my lips to catch on his, sinking into his embrace.

Our time together so far hadn't been dull. In fact, we had faced more obstacles in the few months that we'd been together than any couple should ever need to face in a lifetime.

But I wouldn't trade it for anything. If I had to do it again, I would do it all the same. From the moment that I had screamed at Jesse to pull the car over for the wounded wolf, to standing here in the cemetery toasting my twenty-three years of life, and everything in between.

It made me who I was, who I am. It made me appreciate who my friends were. It opened my eyes to the bigger, albeit a more dangerous, but infinitely more magical world that existed outside of my imagination.

My life wasn't perfect, but I never wanted to take it for granted. I would never wish it away.

For as long as time would allow, I would live my life how I thought that I was meant to be lived, and leave the rest up to fate. I didn't know what was going to happen next week, or next year, or ten years from now, but I did know that I would have Harper beside me and a group of friends that I owed my life to twice over. I made a promise to myself that, each day, I was going to fight like hell to make sure it counted. I couldn't control everything, but I could control my outlook, and I chose to make it a positive one.

The best things in life didn't come easy, so I was sure that things would be hard at times, but I also knew that they would all be worth it.

They already had been.

Such is fate. Such is death. Such is life.

Such is love.